"I'll keep an eye out—you feed your daughter. Unless you're afraid of a baby?"

"I'm not afraid of my daughter." Tuck gathered Lily into his arms and held out his hand for the bottle. "What do I do?"

"Stick it in her mouth. She knows what to do next. All you have to do is hold her."

As he cradled his daughter, a surge of love filled every corner of his soul. Tuck's heart swelled, so he could barely breathe. "She's beautiful." He'd never experienced anything as painfully wonderful as holding his own child in his arms. "Thank you for having her."

"I'm sorry, Tuck. I should have told you about Lily. You had a right to know your daughter. And she had a right to know her father."

Tuck could barely speak. Even with killers waiting for them, he was afraid to ruin this perfect moment.

ELLE JAMES

THUNDER HORSE HERITAGE

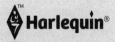
Harlequin®

TORONTO NEW YORK LONDON
AMSTERDAM PARIS SYDNEY HAMBURG
STOCKHOLM ATHENS TOKYO MILAN MADRID
PRAGUE WARSAW BUDAPEST AUCKLAND

This book is dedicated to my writing sprints partner and fellow Harlequin author Gina Wilkins, whose persistence and patience helped me meet my deadline. And I'd also like to dedicate this book to her daughter, who is struggling to rebuild her life after a stroke.

PLEASE RECYCLE
THIS PRODUCT IS RECYCLABLE

Recycling programs
for this product may
not exist in your area.

ISBN-13: 978-0-373-69624-6

THUNDER HORSE HERITAGE

Copyright © 2012 by Mary Jernigan

ABOUT THE AUTHOR

A Golden Heart Award winner for Best Paranormal Romance in 2004, Elle James started writing when her sister issued a Y2K challenge to write a romance novel. She managed a full-time job, raised three wonderful children and she and her husband even tried their hands at ranching exotic birds (ostriches, emus and rheas) in the Texas Hill Country. Ask her, and she'll tell you what it's like to go toe-to-toe with an angry 350-pound bird! After leaving her successful career in information technology management, Elle is now pursuing her writing full-time. She loves building exciting stories about heroes, heroines, romance and passion. Elle loves to hear from fans. You can contact her at ellejames@earthlink.net or visit her website at www.ellejames.com.

Books by Elle James

Other titles by this author available in ebook format.

CAST OF CHARACTERS

Tuck Thunder Horse—Lakota Indian, North Dakota rancher and FBI special agent assigned close to home at the Bismarck, North Dakota, branch office. He didn't believe in love at first sight until it happened to him a year before. Now he doesn't believe in love at all.

Julia Anderson—A schoolteacher who left Tuck on the night of their wedding, who seeks his help to protect her and her daughter.

Lily Anderson—Julia's four-month-old baby girl.

Jillian Anderson—Julia's sister and FBI special agent, who found trouble while visiting Julia.

Ray Mullins—FBI supervisory special agent and Jillian Anderson's boss at regional headquarters in Minneapolis.

Dante Thunder Horse—Tuck's brother, and a helicopter pilot for the North Dakota branch of U.S. Customs and Border Protection.

Pierce Thunder Horse—Tuck's older brother and fellow FBI special agent now assigned to the Bismarck office.

Walter Pickett—National Indian Gambling Commission representative in charge of overseeing the Running Buffalo Casino at Fort Yates.

Timothy Wilks—Casino manager of the Running Buffalo Casino in Fort Yates, North Dakota.

Josh Behling—Tuck's friend and partner at the Bismarck FBI branch office.

Chapter One

Tuck Thunder Horse stared at his phone, debating leaving it off as his plane taxied to the gate in Bismarck, North Dakota. Off duty for the moment, with nothing on his docket but a "rest and recuperate" order to close out his latest FBI assignment, the idea was tempting. And after endless debriefing sessions followed by seven hours in transit from Quantico, Virginia, all he really wanted was to find a bed to fall into.

His sense of responsibility wouldn't let him ignore duty. He switched the phone on and groaned as it immediately started beeping. He had no fewer than five messages and three texts. What could be so all-fired important? His supervisor knew he was on his way back to North Dakota, and his family didn't expect him until later that night. His heartbeat kicked up a notch. Had something happened on the ranch?

Two of the three text messages read "Listen to your voice mail" and were from a buddy of his, Josh Behling, assigned with him to the FBI's Bismarck satellite office. He and Josh went back to initial FBI training at Quantico. Their training days and a few missions that had tested their strength and mettle had forged a friendship that had lasted through the years. He looked forward to seeing his friend.

Behling had promised to meet Tuck at the airport and take him to his apartment, where he'd left his car. Tuck would stay the night there. His brother Pierce would be in from Quantico the following morning. Together they planned to head to the Thunder Horse Ranch, a good three-and-a-half-hour drive, to enjoy their R & R together.

The last text read "911" with a phone number following.

Tuck clicked on the voice mail from Behling, frowning at the three voice mails from a "Blocked Sender." Before Behling's message could begin, his phone buzzed, indicating an incoming call. He hit the talk button.

"Oh, good, you must be on the ground." Behling's voice came over the line, intense, urgent. "I'm here to pick you up, but we've had a change of plan. Do you have a bag to claim?"

"No. I carried it aboard."

The plane pulled to a stop at the gate and the fasten-seat-belt sign blinked off. Passengers filled the aisle, retrieving carry-on baggage from the overhead bins.

Tuck unbuckled and stood, bumping his head on the low storage compartments. Being over six feet tall had its disadvantages on mass transit. He muttered a curse and reached up to grab his suitcase, his hand holding the phone to his ear. "What's the plan?"

"Well…" Josh heaved a sigh. "Sorry to disappoint, but I'm not taking you to your apartment."

"No?" Tuck grinned. "Are we going out on the town for old times' sake?" He inched his way down the aisle toward the hatch, juggling the cell phone against his ear and being careful not to bump the guy in front of him with his case.

"No, we had an agent of the National Indian Gaming Commission murdered tonight. His body was found along the shore of Lake Oahe. We also found a dead woman we haven't identified yet."

Tuck stopped at the door of the plane, his breath lodging in his throat. "Anyone we know?" He'd met a few of the NIGC reps, having dealt with them on occasion over the years.

"No. The guy was covering the casino near Fort Yates. Not sure what's going on down there, but the Sioux County sheriff asked for our help."

At the mention of Fort Yates, a flood of memories crashed over Tuck. The last time he'd been in the town near the South Dakota border, he'd been on a vacation that had ended in total disaster. He sucked in a deep breath as he pushed the memories away and asked, "When did it happen?"

"Don't know yet. I was just getting ready to leave for the site when your plane landed. McGowan's out sick. I need a partner and figured you'd want to be in on the investigation."

"I'm supposed to be off for the next week."

"Yeah," Behling said, "but how often do we have an NIGC murdered in North Dakota?"

"Once in a blue moon."

"Right. Are you in, or do I have to call in our supervisor to cover?"

"I'm on my way. Do we have air transportation available, or are we driving down?"

Behling chuckled. "Got a chopper ready and waiting for us."

"See you out front." Tuck clicked the off button, pocketed his cell phone and sighed. The thought of getting back in the air after having just landed was only slightly more appealing than getting on the road in the opposite direction from the Thunder Horse Ranch. And to be heading to the place he'd sworn off since that fateful night over a year ago… Well, he wasn't exactly thrilled. Yet, he was curious enough to take the bait. Murders in North Dakota came few and far between and…who knew? While he was in Fort Yates, he might run into her. Whoa, now. He pushed that errant thought to the back of his mind.

Behling picked him up outside the airport terminal in his black four-by-four SUV. He didn't wait for Tuck to buckle his belt before he drove away from the curb.

"You mentioned a woman." His chest tightened as he asked, "Who is she?"

Behling glanced in his rearview mirror and merged into the traffic leaving the airport. Before he made it to the airport expressway, he took a turn to the right, heading for the line of hangars where private planes and helicopters parked. "The Sioux County sheriff wasn't forthcoming. He seemed more concerned about the dead commissioner."

"Are we only dealing with the Sioux County Sheriff's Department, or will the Standing Rock Tribal Police be involved, as well?"

"Both. So far they've been cooperative, but I'm not getting much information from them."

Tuck dropped down out of the SUV, and together they entered the building.

"Are you two all that's going?" A man in a navy blue jumpsuit met them at the door to an office, carrying a flight bag and a small clipboard.

"Hi, Rick. We're it." Josh shook hands with the man and turned to Tuck. "Don't know if you two have met. I

had to beg, borrow and steal to get use of this chopper."
He grinned. "Tuck Thunder Horse, meet Rick Knoell."

The men shook hands and headed out to the tarmac,
where a sleek black helicopter sat.

Tuck whistled. "We have the budget for this?"

"Like I said, I had to beg, borrow and steal." Josh
jerked his head toward Rick. "Rick needed some night
flight time. He owed me a favor, and we needed a quick
trip to Fort Yates. It all adds up." He shrugged.

Behling climbed aboard the bird, slipping into the
passenger seat.

Tuck slid into the seat behind him. While Rick performed the preflight check, Tuck listened to his other
voice-mail messages. One from Behling, indicating the
chance of being late to the airport. The other messages
from the blocked sender were nothing but air and an
odd sound like a baby gurgling in the background. Tuck
shook his head. He didn't know anyone with a baby.
Probably a wrong number. But something about the
calls made him uneasy. Why would a wrong number
call back twice?

He didn't have long to worry about it. By the time
he'd deleted the messages, Rick had climbed into the
pilot seat and started the engine.

Once they were in the air, Tuck settled the flight
headset in place over his ears and sat back for the ride,
static and the rumble of the rotors numbing him, creat-
ing white noise in which his thoughts churned.

The last time he'd been to Fort Yates, a little over
a year ago, he'd gone down for a weekend of boating,
gambling and drinking. The memories were a mix of
blurred impressions and startlingly clear images. The
ending of that vacation was not one he'd ever experienced before. After all, it wasn't every day that a man

got engaged, married and ditched all in the span of forty-eight hours, more or less. He still wasn't sure how it had all happened, but he had the pictures and annulment papers that proved it hadn't been a bad dream.

As they neared the small outpost of Fort Yates, the neon lights of the Running Buffalo Casino rose up out of the grasslands, a beacon of garish illumination on the dark prairie. The red, yellow, blue and green neon lights reflected off the still waters of Lake Oahe, a lake formed by a strategically placed dam near Pierre, South Dakota. The lake provided miles of fishing and camping for the residents of North and South Dakota, its shores following the Missouri River's path from Pierre almost to Bismarck.

Tuck's chest tightened as he leaned forward to stare out the window of the helicopter. The casino and the surrounding resort looked just as they had the last time he'd been there. Nothing had changed. Except him. Gone was his carefree, reckless sense of taking each day one at a time. He still didn't know why he'd jumped into the wedding and—more disturbing—why she'd ended it so quickly. The whole situation had made him step back and take stock of his life, and he hadn't much liked the direction he'd been heading.

The helicopter bypassed the casino and landed at the Standing Rock Airport south of town where a Sioux County sheriff's SUV waited, lights flashing on top of the vehicle.

As soon as they exited the chopper, the sheriff met them, his hand held out. "I'm Sheriff White Hawk. I thought you'd never get here."

"Can you bring me up-to-date?" Tuck stepped forward, used to taking charge.

"Our victims were the NIGC rep and a local schoolteacher." The sheriff talked as he led them back to his vehicle. "We cordoned off the shoreline around the two bodies, and I've had a couple of my deputies asking questions around the area. So far, no one saw anything."

Typical. With so much wide-open space in North Dakota, a person could get away with murder, and no one would be the wiser for days. That's where Tuck's job became critical. "Has the state crime-lab team arrived?"

Sheriff White Hawk nodded. "They just got here."

"Was everything left the same way as it was found?"

"Other than the footprints from the fishermen, no one's touched a thing."

"Good." Tuck climbed into the passenger seat of the sheriff's SUV.

They accomplished the short ride to the crime scene in relative silence, the occasional static flaring from the radio on the sheriff's shoulder harness.

A mile past the turnoff to the casino and recreation area, the sheriff turned on a county road, headed toward the lake. After another mile, the lawman slowed the vehicle and glanced at Tuck with a grimace. "We go cross-country from here."

Tuck nodded and held on as they bumped across the dry, flat land to the shore's edge, where several other SUVs and a flotilla of motorboats ringed the crime scene. Yellow crime tape flapped in the wind around the land side of the perimeter.

Tuck ducked beneath the tape and flashed his credentials to get past the battery of Sioux County deputies and Standing Rock tribal policemen.

Once inside the perimeter, Josh hurried forward to the crime-scene technicians and exchanged a few words.

Tuck hung back, his gaze panning the area, his investigative eye noting everything that could be considered evidence. There wasn't much to go on. Based on the lack of blood spatter, the agent and the woman had been murdered elsewhere and their bodies dumped here, probably by boat. The sheriff's deputies would be checking for anyone who might have seen a boat pull close to shore. But as dark as it was, if the boat didn't have a light, no one would have seen a thing.

When Behling stepped back, Tuck caught his first glimpse of the dead woman.

Tuck's breath caught in his throat and his heart jammed in his chest so hard it hurt, a foggy haze settling around the edges of his vision.

Pushing back pain, Tuck sucked in a deep breath, his feet carrying him forward as if he was walking through quicksand. He had to be seeing things that weren't there. It couldn't be her. "Do you have a positive ID on the woman?" he asked, his voice echoing in his head.

The medical examiner looked up at Tuck, his brows raised questioningly. "You have a need to know?"

"It's okay," Behling said. "He's another special agent."

Tuck moved closer, his gaze fixed on the body. "Jesus." He closed his eyes, pressure squeezing his chest tight. "I know her." He opened his eyes and stared down at the lifeless remains of the woman he'd met a little more than a year ago here at Fort Yates.

Behling's head jerked in his direction, his brow furrowing. "You know her?"

Tuck nodded. "That's Julia Anderson. She was my wife."

Chapter Two

An hour later, Tuck sat on the side of the bed in his hotel room at the casino, staring at his hands. What the hell had just happened? He was on his way home for a week off—he'd never planned to spend his vacation finding out who had murdered a woman he'd been married to for a grand total of forty-eight hours.

Behling left him at his door, claiming he had a mound of paperwork and calls to make and that he'd check in with Tuck the next morning when Rick would take them back to Bismarck.

Relieved to have a chance for some time to himself, Tuck had assured Behling he would be fine and needed the rest and an opportunity to think…alone.

Except for the blood staining her chest, Julia looked the same as the last time he'd seen her on their wedding night—what he could remember of it. Long blond hair and pale blue eyes, a slender build, rounded, firm breasts. She'd been a beauty then and was just as beautiful in death. Had they met any other way…had they tried to make their farce of a marriage stick…this scenario might have had a completely different ending.

Over a year had passed since their last correspondence—the annulment papers delivered by courier to his apartment door on his day off.

His head dropped into his open palms, the terrible nature of Julia's death weighing him down. Who had killed her?

The cell phone lying on the bed beside him buzzed. He checked the caller ID—Dante. He didn't bother answering the call. What could Tuck say to his brother? *Hi, I'm in Fort Yates and just got through viewing my ex-wife's remains.*

His brothers didn't even know he'd married. He'd been too embarrassed to tell anyone. He'd been to a bachelor party for a friend and had been so sauced when he'd met Julia, he hadn't been thinking clearly. After dancing with her for two hours straight, they'd ended up in his hotel room, making love until early into the next day. Still high on alcohol and sex, they'd run out to the justice of the peace, obtained a wedding license and tied the knot at the quaint little wedding chapel in Fort Yates. As the alcohol wore off and exhaustion set in, they returned to his hotel room, where they collapsed and slept through the rest of the day and night.

When Tuck had woken the next morning, Julia had been gone, leaving a note with an apology and no forwarding address. She'd filed for an annulment immediately, and their union had been dissolved. Just like that.

When his cell phone quit ringing, Tuck glanced at it, remembering the "911" text message from earlier that day before…well, before everything. Behling's call, the quick trip to Fort Yates and the murders had made him forget to follow through, but now the contents of the message came back to him in a rush.

Could the message have been from Julia? His heart skipped several beats as he dialed the number in the message. Could it have been the last text message Julia had sent before she'd been brutally murdered?

He opened the text screen and a phone number flashed up at him. With a sense of dread, he pressed the number, engaging the dialing capability.

After several rings, someone answered. Or at least Tuck thought someone clicked the talk button. The ringing had stopped, but no one spoke.

"Hello?" Tuck waited in case the connection was bad. Reception in the far reaches of North Dakota was scarce if not nonexistent. "Hello?"

"Tuck? Tuck Thunder Horse?" a feminine voice asked in a whisper.

A hint of recognition tugged at Tuck's consciousness and his heart rate kicked up a notch. "Speaking."

"It's J-Julia."

All the air left Tuck's lungs as if someone had sucker punched him. "Julia?" How could it be Julia? She was dead, her body taken to the Fort Yates morgue. He'd identified the body himself. His stomach gurgled and twisted.

"I need to see you," the woman said.

Tuck ran a hand through his hair. Who the hell was this? Why was she impersonating a dead woman? His grip tightened on the phone as anger forged through him. He tamped it down and feigned ignorance of what he'd witnessed earlier. "When? Where?" His voice was gruffer than he'd intended, a lump knotting in his throat.

"Are you in North Dakota?" she asked.

His lips thinned. "As a matter of fact, I am. Just flew into Bismarck a couple hours ago and made a quick run south to Fort Yates."

She made a noise that sounded suspiciously like a sob. "Oh, thank God."

"Are you all right?" he asked.

"No. No, nothing is all right."

Tuck couldn't agree with her more. Anyone with the gall to pass herself off as a dead woman wasn't firing on all cylinders. "Tell me where you are."

"In Fort Yates." Her words were spoken carefully, as if she was afraid to give away too much.

"Where in Fort Yates? I'll see what I can do to get there."

"I can't tell you. Tell me where you are and I'll meet you."

"I'm at the casino."

After a long pause, she whispered, "Meet me in fifteen minutes at the marina below the casino. Come alone."

Alone. Tuck's sense of self-preservation tensed. She could be setting him up. But for what? Hell, at this point did it matter? He wanted to know her game. "It's dark. How will I find you?"

"Don't worry, I'll find you."

Before he could question her further, the line clicked in his ear.

His emotions still raw from seeing the woman he'd married on a whim lying dead on the shore of Lake Oahe, Tuck's blood ran cold then hot, blazing through his veins like fast-flowing molten lava. How dared she? How dared this stranger call claiming to be Julia, when Julia lay dead?

He checked his watch and headed out the door. The walk to the marina from the hotel wouldn't take long, five minutes max. That would give him ten minutes to watch for her to arrive if she wasn't already there.

His stride ate the distance. Part of him wanted to notify Josh of the phone call, but something in the woman's voice made him hesitate. He had to know her story before he called in his friend, otherwise Behling might think he was imagining things.

Wide-open expanses of North Dakota prairie were interspersed with scrubby little trees along the road down to the marina. Tuck scanned both sides, peering into the bushes and the shadows of the limited vegetation along the way.

The marina consisted of two long jetties jutting out into Lake Oahe with small, medium and large boats moored in the slips. The marina building perched at one end of the pair of jetties, closed for the night, shuttered, with all merchandise displays tucked within the walls. Besides a dirty yellow streetlight on the marina, two lone lights jutted from the top of poles at the end of each jetty, reflecting light off the inky water below.

Tuck had about given up trying to find the woman when a figure detached itself from the shadow of the marina building, a dark cap pulled down low. As Tuck neared the figure, her head turned left then right in a jerky, nervous movement. She wore a long, draping shawl wrapped around her body, disguising her figure. She could have been a young or old woman, fat or thin. He couldn't tell, but he'd find out soon enough.

Tuck stood back, studying the woman for a moment, gathering his nerve and tamping down the desire to strangle her for playing the role of a murder victim.

Coaching himself to calm, he forced all anger from his face and demeanor, then walked forward.

She remained hidden in the shadows.

"I'm here…Julia." His teeth ground together on her name. "What do you want?" Tuck stopped, refusing to move closer. She'd have to meet him halfway.

The hint of a sob drifted across the crisp evening air toward him, and the woman moved another step out of the shadows, her hand reaching out. The glow from the yellowed night light glanced off the side of her face, illuminating her profile.

Tuck sucked in a breath and backed up a step. The female was the image of the one the medical examiner had pronounced dead only a short while ago.

Tuck lurched forward, gripping her arms, his fingers digging in, refusing to let her escape. "Who the hell are you?"

She hunched her shoulders, her body shaking, staring up at him, searching his face. "Tuck?" His name wasn't so much a question as a statement, and some of the tension in her arms slackened.

Tuck's grip tightened. He'd be ready if she tried to make a run for it.

"We can't stay here," she whispered.

Tuck's eyes narrowed. "We're not going anywhere until you answer my question…here…now." His jaw tightened and he refused to move.

Her gaze darted left then right. "We're not safe."

He snorted. "Should have thought of that before you chose this spot."

"I had to be sure it was you before…"

"Before what?"

"Please, could we go somewhere safe, not so out in the open?" She tugged against his grip, her gaze darting past him.

"Who are you afraid of?" Tuck demanded.

"I don't know." She stared up at him, her blue eyes wide, frightened. "Please, we have to go somewhere safe."

"We can stay here or go to my room at the casino." His mouth pressed into a thin line. He was reluctant to let this woman into his room, but curiosity burned too strongly to ignore. He had to know who she was and what was going on.

"Your room?" Again her gaze darted left then right, and she ducked her head. "No, I can't," she said, her voice cracking. "I can't go back there."

"We don't have many choices in a town the size of Fort Yates. Do you have any other suggestions?"

"I can't go home." Her body drooped, her arms going limp. "I have nowhere else to go."

Tuck hesitated another second, then let go of one of her arms, keeping a tight hold on the other as he led her back the way he'd come, toward the hotel casino. He berated himself inwardly for falling into her plan, but if he wanted to get to the bottom of this charade, he had to play along until he got answers.

As they neared the hotel, she slowed, adjusted the bulky shawl around her middle, bringing the fabric high around her neck. With shaking hands, she tugged the hat lower over her eyes, pushing long, loose strands of hair back under the hat's rim.

Past being patient, Tuck nudged her forward with a little more force than he intended and stepped up on the back porch of the casino, pushing through the double glass doors to the stairwell.

The shawl-wrapped female stumbled. A small cry burst from beneath the shawl, but it didn't sound as if it came from the woman.

"What the hell?" Tuck reached out to yank the shawl aside.

A hand whipped out, knocking his aside. Blue eyes stared up at him, sandy-blond brows diving like daggers toward the bridge of her nose. "Don't."

"I'm not taking you into the hotel until I know what

you're hiding beneath that shawl." He reached out again for the shawl.

She stepped back, her chin tightening, her eyes narrowing to slits. "And I'm telling you if you try to remove the shawl, I'll kill you." To emphasize her point, she jabbed him in the side with the business end of a revolver. "Now, are we going to your room or what?"

Tuck's pulse leaped. If he wasn't mistaken, the gun appeared to be a SIG Sauer revolver, just like the one he carried on duty with the FBI. Unfortunately, his was at the armory. Headed for a week off, he hadn't seen the need to carry. What the hell was she doing with a SIG Sauer? The way she held the revolver was a sure sign she had no clue how to use it, but that didn't make the weapon any less deadly. He remained calm. "Aren't you afraid someone will see you holding a gun?"

"No." Even after her arm came to a stop, the bulk around her middle shifted. "Now, are you going to take me to your room, or do I have to use this?"

He didn't move, gauging whether or not she had the gumption to pull the trigger. Now more than curious about her story, he decided to go along with her plan. If necessary, he could easily disarm her when the time came. "Come on."

She let out a breath. "Good. The sooner we get this meeting over with, the better."

"You're tellin' me." He led the way up the stairs to the third floor. When they reached his door, Tuck inserted the key and waited for her to enter.

As she passed across the threshold, she turned to face him, the gun tenting the shawl. "Don't try anything. I know how to use this. And I really don't want to."

"I don't doubt that in the least," Tuck lied, following her into the room.

Once he had the door closed firmly behind him, he faced the woman, his heart stone cold. "Now that we're alone, suppose you tell me why the hell a *dead* woman is holding me at gunpoint."

JULIA GASPED, HER HEART squeezing so tightly in her chest she couldn't breathe. "Shut up."

"Who are you?" Tuck Thunder Horse stalked toward her, closing the distance between them. "I watched the coroner zip the body bag on Julia Anderson."

Julia raised her empty hand to her ear, tears filling her eyes. "Shut up," she whispered. She'd suspected her sister was already dead, but having it confirmed stole her breath away. Her body trembled, the tremors becoming more violent until she shook so hard she could barely stand. "Shut up."

"No. I will not shut up until you tell me what's going on."

Julia swallowed hard, knowing that in order to keep herself and her baby safe, she had to hold it together. Had to get Tuck Thunder Horse to take her and Lily into his protection, or they'd die before she could get them away from Fort Yates.

Die just like her twin sister.

"I *am* Julia Anderson. You and I were married over a year ago. I filed for an annulment the next day." A lump of emotion lodged in her throat. Her sister lay on a cold, hard slab in the morgue. She'd already lost one of the only two people she had left in this world. She'd be damned if she let anyone hurt Lily. And Tuck was the only one she trusted to help protect her baby.

Tuck's jaw tightened, a tic flickering in the left side. "If you're Julia, then who the hell was in the body bag?"

The baby wrapped snugly against Julia's belly stirred

and whimpered. Lily, sweet Lily, the love of her life, her reason for living.

Julia coughed to cover the sound of the child's whimper. "That was my twin sister, Jillian. Whoever killed her will be after me next."

"What?" Tuck shoved a hand through his hair, her revelation hitting home. He really hadn't known anything about Julia when he'd married her. "You expect me to believe you had a twin?"

Julia jerked the hat from her head and let her long blond hair fall down around her shoulders. She and her sister had been identical twins, Jillian arriving two minutes before Julia. Their mother had told them that Jillian had arrived kicking and screaming, Julia in a more sedate manner, calm and angelic. "Did she look just like me?"

The man studied her face, his gaze traveling from the tip of her head down the length of her body. "Hard to say when you're covered from head to foot."

Julia dropped the hat on the floor and slid her free hand beneath the shawl. Patting the bundle around her middle, she hesitated, reluctant to spring the next shock on a man who already didn't trust a word she said. "Well, it's true. We were sisters." The ready tears sprang to her eyes, and she dashed them away with the edge of the shawl.

"Do you know what happened to her?" Tuck asked, his voice hard.

Julia nodded.

"Do you know why?" he asked next.

"Yes. That's why I called you."

"Why me? Why contact me after all this time?"

She drew in a long, steadying breath. The time had come to tell him the rest of the story. "We need help."

"We? Seems a little late for your sister."

Julia winced, actually hating this man for a minute for his callousness. Still, maybe it was better that he could be so calm, so detached. Heaven knew she couldn't—not with so much at stake. Her sister was dead. She could be next. Her baby was at risk. All of that meant she had to convince Tuck to protect them. "*I'm* in trouble and need help."

"What makes you think I'll help you?" He glared at her. "You didn't want anything to do with me a year ago. You didn't even have the decency to say goodbye."

Guilt lay heavily on Julia's heart, but the strong sense of protectiveness she'd developed since the birth of her daughter won out. Protecting her daughter was more important to her than anything. For Lily's sake, she would take whatever harsh words this man chose to throw at her. Besides, she knew she deserved them. Sneaking out of the hotel room, running off with no explanation and ending their marriage long-distance, without laying eyes on the man again... It had been a weak, cowardly thing to do. She knew that. But now she had no choice but to be brave—for her baby's sake, if not for her own.

With a deep, indrawn breath, Julia laid the gun on the television console and, grasping the corner of the shawl, lifted it up over her head, dropping it to the floor.

For several seconds, Tuck studied her, his brow furrowing. He didn't move, didn't speak, just stared at her middle.

Then Lily moved, a tiny hand peeking out from the fabric of the sling, waving in the air.

"Tuck Thunder Horse, I'm sorry I didn't tell you sooner, but meet Lily." Julia swallowed hard and continued, "Your baby girl."

Chapter Three

All the air left Tuck's lungs in a whoosh, and the image of the baby wavered like a mirage on hot desert terrain.

As quickly as his vision blurred, anger raged, red-hot and fiery, erupting through his body. "How dare you threaten me—with a gun *or* a baby. Do you really expect me to believe that this baby is mine?" He poked a finger at the woman's chest. "Even if you're telling the truth about your twin and you really are Julia, why should that make me trust you? You weren't all that trustworthy when you married me and then walked out on me less than a day later. Do you think I'm stupid enough to believe anything you have to say to me?"

She hugged the child to her chest and then loosened her hold, titling her forward so that Tuck could see her face.

Nestled in a pink fluffy blanket, the infant's mouth moved in a soft sucking motion, her shock of thick black hair stealing Tuck's anger, sucking the fire right out of his veins.

"She looks like you," Julia whispered. "She has your hair, your dark skin…your eyes." Just as she said the words, the baby blinked up at him with dark orbs, already losing their baby blue for the ink-black so typical of the Thunder Horse family's Lakota heritage.

Tuck's chest squeezed so tightly, he could barely draw in air. The baby did look like him. "So, she has black hair." He fought the urge to reach out and touch the baby's rosy cheek. "That doesn't mean she's mine."

"She's four months old." Julia stared across the baby at him. "You do the math." His ex-wife reached around her neck with one hand and fumbled with the knot holding the sling, while balancing the baby in her other arm. When she had the sling loose, she handed the child across to Tuck.

He hesitated and drew back, his hands dropping to his sides.

"Hold her. She won't bite." Julia shoved the baby at him, giving him no choice but to take the squirming bundle.

He grasped the baby, holding her out like an alien being. Then Tuck stared at the infant girl, who stared back at him, her dark hair and dark eyes so very much like his own.

Then she smiled, the mere quirk of those tiny lips and cherubic cheeks nearly bringing Tuck to his knees.

His hands shook. Rather than drop the baby, he brought her close to his body and cradled her against his chest. "Are you sure?" Tuck glanced up at the woman standing across from him.

Julia's lips trembled, her eyes glistening with tears. "Never more certain."

"Why didn't you tell me?"

She sighed. "I didn't know I was pregnant until two months after we met…and then it snowballed, all happening so quickly." She gulped, her head dipping low. "One minute I was a single woman with no cares in the world, the next I was scrambling to find a place big enough for a baby. The school semester started. I was working teaching kids. A lot of things were happening at once."

"And it just slipped your mind? You never thought for a moment that I had a right to know?"

"Yes, you did." Her belly twisted with her guilt. "I didn't know whether or not you'd want to be a part of her life." It was just an excuse, but it was the one she'd clung to, so that she wouldn't have to get back in touch with the man she'd married and then run away from. So she'd made the choice for him.

"And you made the decision not to tell me." He shook his head.

"After what happened between us, I thought it would be unfair to saddle you with a child you might not want." She sighed. "I was wrong."

She'd been wrong about so many things.

Marrying Tuck in the first place had been a mistake. Even now, she could hardly believe she'd done it. It was so unlike her to get carried away, swept off her feet. Jillian had always been the spontaneous one—not Julia. Julia was the thinker, the planner, the one who calculated cost and consequence for every decision she made.

If she'd taken the time to stop and think, she never would have gone to that little wedding chapel. She'd have taken the time to get to know her husband first— at least well enough to know what he did for a living. If she'd been aware before saying her vows that he was an FBI agent, then she would have realized that a relationship between them could never work.

Julia knew all too well what being an agent meant. Her father had spent most of her formative years away from home as a member of the bureau. She recalled how her mother had waited by the telephone every time he was on assignment, expecting the call that her husband had been injured or killed in the line of duty. Sadly, she'd gotten that call when Julia and Jillian were twelve years old.

Jillian had followed their father into the FBI.

Julia still couldn't understand why her sister would do such a thing, knowing the dangers. Hadn't losing a parent shown her how dangerous it was?

Julia had never considered joining the FBI or having anything to do with it. The job hadn't just taken her father away from her—it had ruined her mother's life, as well. Julia had seen the way the stress and anxiety of being an agent's wife had weighed on her mother. It was a strain Julia refused to bear. Bad enough that she had to worry about her sister on the job. She refused to worry about a husband, too.

When she'd found Tuck's badge in the hotel room, she'd lost it. Images of her mother trying not to cry as she sat by the phone had flooded her memories, bringing her to her knees on the bedroom floor of the hotel. She couldn't get away from Tuck fast enough. She refused to be one of those wives who waited night and day for "the call."

All Julia had wanted was a safe home with someone who would be there to love her. A father who put his family ahead of his work. A man who wasn't destined to die of gunshot wounds earned in the line of duty.

Just a glimpse of that all-too-familiar badge had been enough to make Julia run. She'd departed the hotel, leaving a note that she was sorry and that their marriage had been a mistake. Annulment papers had been easy to obtain, and within forty-eight hours she wasn't married.

Of course, there were still consequences she never could have anticipated. Consequences like the precious baby girl cradled for the first time in her father's arms.

For a long time he stared down at the baby. "I have a daughter." He shook his head, his eyes widening. "I have a daughter. What did you say her name was?"

"Lily. Lily Amelia." She looked down at her hands. "You said your mother's name was Amelia. I thought it was pretty."

She'd named his daughter after his mother. Tuck touched a finger to the baby's rounded cheek, marveling at how soft and smooth her skin was. "You had no right," he whispered. The baby had been born four months ago. Four months he could have been getting to know her. "You had no right to keep her from me."

"Agreed."

Anger and regret made a resurgence through him. "Then why?" He glared at her. "Why now? There must be something you want, or you wouldn't have contacted me."

Julia stepped forward. "Like I said, we need your help. We're in trouble."

"The same trouble that took your sister's life?"

She flinched, her lips trembling. "Yes."

"Who was behind the murder?"

"I don't know. My sister and I had gone to the casino. She was on vacation, visiting me." Julia swallowed hard before she could continue, her words coming out in a rush. "Jillian was making a video of me on the path outside the casino—the one that leads to the marina. She wanted to get the lake in the background. I was turning to get in a better position when I saw movement by the docks."

She pressed a hand to her mouth, her eyes widening. "When I looked closer, I could see a man being held at gunpoint and then shot in the chest down by the water. Jillian caught it all on her camera without realizing what was happening. I was too shocked to say anything. It happened so fast." She stared up at Tuck, all the horror she must have witnessed reflecting in her watery blue eyes. "But then the murderer glanced our way. I don't think he saw Jillian, but he definitely saw me."

Tuck's hands tightened around the baby. "What happened?"

"I told my sister." Julia's head moved back and forth as if she were in a daze. "She went after him."

"Where were you?"

"She made me promise to go home and wait for her. To take care of Lily until Jillian came for me." She stopped talking, tears dripping down off her chin. "My sister never came back." Julia's words thickened. "God, I shouldn't have let her go." Her eyes filled with tears and overflowed, rivulets of grief running down her face.

With the baby in his arms, Tuck could do nothing to comfort her. Nor should he want to, given their history together. She'd lied by omission. Something as important as a child of his own wasn't a fact you kept from a father.

Besides, she hadn't come to him for comfort—she'd come to him for help. She'd said she was in trouble, and it was up to him to get to the bottom of it. "Did you notify the authorities about your situation?"

"Yes, I called you."

"No, I mean did you call the sheriff?"

"No."

"Why the hell not?"

Julia gave him a watery smile. "Because Jillian told me not to. I never saw my sister after I left her in front of the casino, but I *did* hear from her one more time. I was waiting at home when I got a text message. The attachment was the video Jillian made of the murder. It's just enough someone with the right equipment might be able to make out the murderer. The message told me to take Lily and run—and not to trust anyone, not even the police, and definitely not the FBI."

"Dam—" Tuck clamped his lips closed, frowned and held out the baby. "Maybe you'd better take her."

"She's yours." Julia stepped back, her hands held up in surrender.

"And yours." He continued to hold the child out to Julia. "Take her."

Lily whimpered, squirming in Tuck's hands.

"You're scaring her." Julia hesitated, her arms rising then falling to her sides. "Please. You hold her. I feel so shaky right now, I'd probably scare her even more." She dug in a pocket and pulled out her phone, her hands trembling so badly, she almost dropped it. "She must have sent the text as she was…d-dying. Why wouldn't she trust anyone in law enforcement? My sister works… worked for the FBI. She was a special agent, like you."

Tuck's brows rose. "Your sister was FBI?"

"Yes." She looked down at the floor, but not before he had a chance to see that her blue eyes were glazed with unshed tears.

Her grief tugged at Tuck's heart, when he had no business reacting to anything about her. He didn't know her, other than the one night they'd spent in bed. One night.

Apparently, one night was all it took. His gaze shifted to the baby in his arms. He was amazed by the fact he was a father. One night, and a beautiful baby was conceived.

Lily's dark eyes blinked up at him. She looked so much like a Thunder Horse, it hurt to think of her in any kind of danger. Tuck's jaw hardened. "Let me call a friend of mine and see what's happening with the investigation. We'll take it from there. But I'm not making any promises."

Julia's eyes widened. "You won't tell them about me and Lily?"

"I won't say a word." He hugged Lily close to his chest. A wave of protectiveness made his arm tighten around the tiny bundle. He'd do anything to keep this child safe.

"Are you sure you can trust the man you're about to call?" Julia chewed on her lower lip, the movement capturing Tuck's attention. She was so beautiful, with her blond hair and blue eyes.

"I'd trust him with my life."

She leveled her gaze at him. "What about the life of your baby?"

His baby. The words struck him all over again. The tiny human in his arms was his child, a part of him and completely dependent on him to protect her from harm. The baby's eyes drifted shut, her cheek resting against his chest, trusting him to keep her safe and warm. "I trust him," he repeated. Josh had saved him on more than one occasion, and Tuck had returned the favor. They were as tight as brothers.

Julia nodded, gathered Lily from his arms and walked around the small living area, gently rocking the baby back to sleep.

Still in a state of semishock, Tuck dialed Josh's personal cell phone and waited, his gaze on the woman and baby who'd completely rocked his world. The phone was answered on the second ring. "Josh?"

"Yeah, Tuck."

"Anything new on the murder case?"

"I just got off the phone with Bismarck. I can't go

into a lot of detail, but it's never good when we lose an NIGC. They want answers, and fast."

"Typical. Got any leads on who did it?" Tuck asked.

"No, and from what the sheriff said, we don't have any live witnesses."

Tuck glanced across at Julia. The one witness they had was too afraid to come out of hiding, the only other evidence on a cell-phone video.

His blood ran cold. That put Julia right in the middle of the investigation. If the killer knew that Jillian had sent Julia that video, he'd do anything to eliminate all eyewitnesses and destroy any physical evidence. And he might be ruthless enough to use a baby to get what he wanted.

"What about the Anderson woman?" he asked.

Julia's attention swung back to him, her eyes wide.

"That's the sad part. She was identified as a local schoolteacher. All we can figure is that she witnessed the murder and was killed for her trouble. Strange thing is that there were no signs of a struggle."

"None?"

"No. And unlike the NIGC rep, who was shot, the woman was stabbed. She might have known the killer. We checked in at her apartment, and the neighbors said she had a baby, which is strange."

"How so?" Tuck asked.

"The babysitter who lives next door said Julia picked the kid up around the same time as the murder. The murderer could have killed her close to her apartment, but no one's seen the baby since. We have an Amber Alert out. I hope the killer doesn't have her." Josh sighed. "It's tragic when the innocent become collateral damage."

Tuck knew exactly where the baby was, but he

clamped his lips shut, not ready to reveal any more than he had to. "Anything else?"

"Yeah, the babysitter mentioned a sister who came to visit. There's a suitcase and clothing, but we haven't located the sister, and there wasn't any identification in her belongings. Maybe she's taken off with the baby, running scared. We've initiated a background check to see if we can locate the sister."

"Let me know what you find."

Josh snorted. "Man, you're supposed to be off. I'm sorry I dragged you all the way down here."

"Yeah, but I knew the victim. Now I've got a stake in this."

"We meeting for breakfast in the morning?" Josh asked.

"Sorry, Josh. I think I'll sleep in. That little bit of jet lag is kicking in. But call me if you learn anything else or if Rick wants to leave early." Tuck's gaze met Julia's. The dark smudges beneath her eyes and the tears trembling on her lashes made his chest ache. When he clicked the off key, he stood for a long moment, his world having made a one-eighty.

"You didn't tell him I was here. Does that mean you're going to help us?" She hugged Lily closer. "Because if you aren't, I'm out of here."

"Fort Yates won't be safe once the killer figures out there's another witness. You better hope he didn't find your sister's phone."

Either way, Tuck knew that Julia would be in danger by morning, if she wasn't already. Once the forensics team did their job, it wouldn't be long before they discovered the dead woman was really Jillian Anderson. Whoever had killed her would put two and two together after it came out that Jillian had a twin named Julia, alerting the killer to the possibility that the woman who witnessed his crime and the woman who came after him were two separate people. And God forbid he'd found Jillian's phone. It would show that her last communication was to send Julia the video with evidence of the murder. He'd be after Julia, and Lily would no longer be safe if she stayed with her mother.

She drew in a deep breath and looked down at the baby sleeping in her arms. "I have to get Lily out of Fort Yates."

"First thing in the morning. Right now, you look dead on your feet." As soon as the words left his mouth, he could have bitten his tongue.

The ready tears spilled from her eyes, running down her wan cheeks. "I'm sorry. I just can't seem to stop crying."

"Understandable. You just lost your sister." The thought of losing one of his brothers hit Tuck so hard that before he could think straight, he pulled Julia and his baby into his arms and held them. The fear of what might happen to them outweighed the fear of losing his heart all over again.

Yeah, his life had just gotten a whole lot more complicated.

Julia lay awake in the king-size bed of the hotel suite, Lily sleeping quietly beside her.

Through the crack in the bedroom door, she watched Tuck moving around. The coolly efficient FBI agent was worlds away from the funny, attentive, passionate man she'd met and married a year before.

Her life had come full circle—not just bringing her back to Tuck, but also landing her last adult relative in the morgue. The career path that had frightened her all her life, that had taken away her father, broken her mother's heart and driven her away from Tuck all those months ago, was now the reason why she'd turned to Tuck for protection. She trusted him to keep her and Lily safe. But what would happen when all of this was over? He knew about Lily now, and if the look on his face when he held the baby was any indication, he wouldn't let Julia just walk away with his child again.

She really didn't know anything about Tuck, his family, where he grew up, what his parents were like. He'd mentioned his mother, but did he have siblings? Were they anything like him? Would they want to know Lily? They hadn't had time in their whirlwind courtship to find out all the important details.

What if Tuck wasn't a fit father for Lily? Julia would take Lily and raise her all by herself if that's what it took.

But what if he *was* every inch the good man he seemed to be? If he was capable of being a good father, then she had no right to keep him from his daughter. Yet could she let him become part of their lives without developing feelings for him? Feelings that would place her right in her mother's shoes, spending all her life worrying over him all the time?

In the outer room, Tuck unbuttoned the blue chambray shirt he wore and let it slide down over his back.

Julia's breath caught in her chest.

Tall, broad shoulders, swarthy skin, hair hanging down almost to his shoulders, he could have been in a commercial promoting the Lakota Indians of the Dakotas, or an extra in a Wild West movie.

No wonder she'd fallen in bed with him. What single woman wouldn't want to? It was hardly surprising she'd been too caught up in the moment to think of taking necessary precautions. She looked down at the sleeping bundle nestled at her side. She couldn't regret, even for a moment, anything that brought her daughter into her life. But still, she knew she could have handled the situation much better.

During her pregnancy, she'd struggled with the truth, knowing she should tell Tuck about the pregnancy. Julia knew it really boiled down to Tuck's work with the FBI. She'd been determined to raise Lily on her own, proving she didn't need a man, especially one who was in such a dangerous line of work.

Guilt lodged like a twisted sock in her belly. She should have told him. He had every right to see his daughter. He could have been there for her when Lily had been born. Maybe things would have worked out for them. Tuck might be luckier than her father and sister. He might live to see his own grandchildren brought into this world.

Sure, and pigs can fly.

Pain washed over her anew. What more proof did she need? Her FBI agent father had died in the line of duty. Her sister worked for the FBI, and now she was dead. More tears welled in Julia's eyes.

Tuck sat on the sofa and pulled his cowboy boots off. Then he stood and unbuttoned his jeans.

Julia should have turned away and allowed him his privacy, but she couldn't. Her tears continued to slide down her cheeks, even as her gaze was drawn to the agent like a moth to a flame.

He loosened the button, his fingers grasping the zipper, then he paused. As if he thought better of it, his hands dropped to his sides and he glanced toward the bedroom.

Julia squeezed her eyes shut, feigning sleep.

The soft shuffle of bare feet on carpet let her know he'd entered the bedroom.

Carefully, Julia peeked through her lashes.

Tuck Thunder Horse leaned over the bed, staring down at the baby beside her. He reached out and brushed a finger over her cheek, his dark eyes fathomless, his square jaw rigid.

He bent and brushed a kiss across Lily's forehead. His gaze shifted to Julia, his expression unreadable. As quietly as he'd entered the room, he moved on to the bathroom.

Julia's gaze followed his retreating figure, an uncomfortable twinge of jealousy making her wish she'd been the one to receive the kiss, recalling how nice his lips felt on hers so long ago.

She shook her head, forcing her thoughts to clear. She couldn't let herself fall into her attraction for Tuck again. This situation was temporary, just until the danger was resolved.

Her damp cheeks reminded her of what was glaringly important in this scenario. Her sister was dead, and she and Lily might be next.

Chapter Four

Tuck turned on the shower faucet, leaving it on a cool setting.

Sleep was the furthest thing from his mind with his ex-wife lying in the bedroom on the other side of the door. His groin tightened, memories of their fateful night together causing blood to flow and surge down low. A cold shower had been the only remedy he could pursue. Sleeping with Julia was not even a possibility. Not after she'd skipped out on him after their wedding night and omitted informing him of such a significant event as the birth of his child.

Anger at himself for still being so drawn to her burned along with the lust in his veins. Tuck stepped into the shower, the cool water pelting his skin, barely dampening the desire building inside. He grabbed for the miniature bottle of shampoo and scrubbed his hands through his hair, digging in his fingers hard enough to scrape his scalp. Yet, no amount of rubbing would rid his mind of her scent, her porcelain skin, the silken blond hair, the gentle swell of her hips, the full, sensuous lips—everything that made her Julia.

Tuck groaned, his soap-covered hands slipping down his torso to the hard erection he couldn't shake by willpower or chilled water.

How was he supposed to keep her safe, when all he wanted was to lose himself in her body?

He forced himself to visualize the baby sleeping beside her. The dark-haired female version of himself lying so peacefully beside her mother, unaware of the danger she faced. The gravity of Lily's situation was better at pulling him out of his fog of desire than being doused in icy water.

The baby gave him the necessary resolve to pull his head out of his lust and focus on the situation at hand. No matter what he wanted or desired, the baby was his main concern. Keeping Lily—and her mother—out of harm's way had to be his focus. The only way to keep them safe was by catching the man who'd killed the NIGC representative and Julia's sister.

He'd seen the video. The distance from the subject and the graininess made it difficult to determine the identity of the shooter. With advanced techniques and equipment, they had a chance. *If* he could get Julia, Lily and the cell phone out of Fort Yates intact.

JULIA LAY BESIDE LILY, staring at the ceiling, unable to sleep with the sound of the shower on the other side of the bathroom door. Tuck would be standing naked beneath the spray. As if it was only yesterday, she recalled standing in a similar shower in this very hotel over a year ago with Tuck Thunder Horse, admiring her husband's strong, sexy body, her fingers roving, exploring, her tongue tasting and memorizing every inch of the Native American.

Her pulse quickened, her blood burning a course straight to her core. She hadn't taken a lover since that night—even before she found out she was pregnant. She'd just known that no other man would make her feel the way Tuck had. While her marriage had been brief, those hours she'd spent in Tuck's arms had been electric, overpowering—above and beyond anything she'd ever known. Had she been too rash running out on Tuck before giving their crazy marriage a chance?

The thought of her sister lying in a cold, dark morgue brought her back to reality with a dull thud against her bruised heart. No, she had been right to leave and avoid falling deeper in love with the man. Had she stayed with him, she'd have set herself up to suffer the similar heartache of having lost her father and sister to the bureau.

She'd seen what it had done to her mother, watched her as over the years she'd withered away, dying by inches every day her husband was on active duty and then fading slowly of a broken heart once she'd lost him.

The sudden buzzing of her cell phone jerked Julia out of her morose thoughts and back to the present. She grabbed for the device and stared at the screen display. "Blocked Sender."

Julia sat up and glanced at the bathroom door. Should she answer or let it ring? She wished Tuck would walk out at that moment and tell her what to do. But the shower continued on.

After the third ring, Lily woke and let out a cry.

Her nerves jangled by the evening's events and Lily's cries, Julia couldn't think straight. She pressed the talk button and held the phone to her ear, her heart stopping, her vocal cords frozen in her throat.

"Julia Anderson, everyone thinks you're dead. But I know the truth." The raspy voice growled into Julia's ear. "I also know what your sister sent you, before she died."

"I d-don't k-know what you're talking about," Julia lied.

"I have her cell phone. I know about the video file.

If you don't keep the file to yourself and give me your cell phone, you and your baby will end up just like her."

Julia's hand shook so badly, the phone slipped from her fingers and fell to the floor. As if Lily sensed her distress, her whimpers amplified into wails.

Tears welled in Julia's eyes and she stumbled to her feet, staring down at the device at her feet as if it was a snake coiled to strike.

"What's wrong?" Tuck stood in the now-open doorway of the bathroom, a towel slung around his hips, water dripping off his body, pooling at his feet.

"The phone," Julia answered in a stupor.

Tuck's jaw tightened. "Whose phone?"

"Mine." She glanced down at the seemingly innocuous phone at her feet.

"You didn't answer it, did you?"

She nodded, her gaze shifting back to Tuck.

A tic jerked in his jaw, his lips firming into a thin line. "The killer?"

She nodded.

"What did he say?"

"He'll kill Lily and me if I share the video with anyone." Julia lifted the baby off the bed and hugged her close to her chest.

"So he knows about Jillian and that she sent the clip to you." Tuck's words were a statement. He reached back into the bathroom and grabbed his jeans. "We need to get out of here."

Her breath catching in her throat, Julia whispered, "Now?"

Lily whimpered.

Tuck stared across at Julia, his expression as hard as his jaw. "Now. Pack fast."

He strode into the living area of the suite, dropped the towel and slid his legs into his jeans.

For a moment, Julia could only stare at his naked backside, her mouth gone dry. Then she spun into action, her child's safety crystallizing as the most important thing in her mind. She laid Lily on the bed and blocked her in on each side by pillows before getting dressed and then stuffing diapers, bottles and formula into her backpack.

In less than two minutes Julia had everything. As she tied the sling around her neck, she glanced across at Tuck, who stood at the window, peering around the edge of the curtain.

TUCK HAD HIS SUITCASE waiting by the door. He checked out the window to see if any new cars had shown up in the parking lot below. As late as it was, most gamblers had either called it a night and gone to bed or were spending the night at a slot machine, hoping to hit the big jackpot. Nothing moved in the parking lot.

Then a couple of pairs of headlights shone down the long drive leading into the casino.

His pulse quickening, Tuck zeroed in on the vehicles, calling out over his shoulder, "It's time to move."

"I'm ready." Julia appeared at his side, Lily wrapped around her middle as she'd been before, the shawl draped over her body. Julia leaned over his arm and stared out. "What's going on down there?"

"I have no intentions of finding out. Let's get out of here." He grabbed his suitcase and then set it down, thinking better of it. Nothing in it was that important. He'd move faster without it. He took Julia's backpack from her, then he held the door open for the mother and child.

After Julia passed through, he caught up and moved around her, heading for the stairs, not the elevator. He took the steps two at a time, arriving at the bottom first.

Julia maneuvered the stairwell at a slower pace, careful not to slip and fall with her precious cargo.

Tuck opened the door leading out the back of the building and checked for bad guys. "The coast is clear for now. But we need to move fast."

"Where are we going?" Julia started to push past him to the outside.

Tuck spotted movement at the corner of the building. A man in dark clothing rounded the corner, his head swiveling back and forth, searching.

For Julia, no doubt. Tuck jerked her back into the building and pushed her behind the metal staircase. "Wait here beneath the stairs until I come back. Keep down and keep quiet."

He ducked out the door, sliding into the shadows of a nearby bush. As he inched his way along the wall of the casino building, he kept the man in view while searching for a way to get Julia out of the hotel and away safely.

Tuck spotted a golf cart near the back entrance, parked beneath an awning.

About that time, the man searching the back of the building moved abreast of where Tuck hid in the shadows. In the meager light from the moonless night, the dark silhouette of a pistol was clearly visible. Tuck didn't recognize the man as any of the sheriff's deputies, the tribal policemen who'd been at the murder scene earlier or the potential witnesses he had questioned at the casino.

The man wore dark clothes and moved in a crouched stance, easing through the darkness like someone who'd done this before. Making a snap judgment, Tuck darted out, knocked the gun from the man's hand and jabbed an elbow up into the guy's nose.

He doubled over at the same time as Tuck's knee came up, connecting with his face. The guy fell to the earth and lay still.

Knowing he might have only moments before the man regained consciousness and raised an alarm, Tuck ran for the golf cart and felt in the dark, praying for a key. When his fingers closed around the hard metal, he sent a silent prayer to *Wakantanka,* the Great Spirit. He cranked the engine and slammed into Reverse, backed all the way to the rear door of the casino and motioned for Julia.

She hurried out, sliding into the passenger seat even as Tuck whipped the cart into Forward and sped toward the marina.

"What happened to the man you saw?" Julia spun around in her seat, checking behind them.

"Taken care of," Tuck said between gritted teeth as the cart bounced down the narrow lane to the marina by the lake.

"Where are we going? Shouldn't we be looking for a getaway car or something?"

"Not a car. We're going by boat. The drive into the casino is narrow. They'll spot us immediately. The lake is big enough to give us a lead on them."

Julia held on to the brace bar the canopy was mounted on as Tuck pushed the little cart to the limit. "I think someone's following us. Make that two people." She turned to Tuck. "Can you make this thing go faster?"

Tuck's teeth ground together. He had the accelerator floored. "This is as good as it gets, unless you think you can run faster, carrying Lily."

"No way. But they're gaining on us."

A quick glance behind him assured Tuck. "We'll get there first." Then luck would have to be with them. The first boat they came to had to have the key in the ignition, or they'd be sitting ducks.

Lily whimpered.

Tuck didn't dare glance down at her. He had to make it to the marina and get them the hell away before anything happened.

A dull thump made the cart shudder. Bits of hard plastic splintered across Tuck's back. "Get down!"

Hanging on to the seat, Julia slid onto the floorboard of the cart, her free arm clutched around Lily's form. "They're shooting at us," she cried. "What if they hit Lily?"

"Not gonna happen." Tuck hoped he was right. He bumped up onto the wooden pier, barely slowing as he took stock of the moored boats.

A long, sleek jet boat caught his attention. He aimed the cart in that direction and floored the accelerator again. The cart leaped forward, bumping over the wooden planks, jarring the occupants.

Lily's voice rose in a wail, her cry matched by Julia's as she tumbled out of the cart backward, landing flat on her back on the pier in front of the jet boat.

"Julia?" Tuck feared she'd fallen in, but there was no splash.

Julia waved a hand. "We're okay, just shaken."

"Stay put." Tuck jumped out of the cart and dived into the jet boat. He groped for the ignition switch, praying the owner had been stupid enough to leave it there. "Damn." No key.

He hopped out and into the ski boat beside it. A fat foam miniature buoy dangled from a key in the ignition. Tuck glanced up the path toward the casino. The silhouettes of three men raced toward them.

"Get in!" Tuck revved the engine, leaned over the side and unhooked the ropes tying the boat to the dock.

In seconds Julia was on her feet, racing for the boat.

Tuck reached out to capture her beneath her arms and swung her and Lily into the boat.

A soft popping sound was followed by wooden splinters flying off the dock into Tuck's face. He ducked low and shifted the boat into Reverse, pulling the lever all the way back. The ski boat roared out of the slip, backing away from the marina as fast as Tuck could make it go. When they were well away from the shooters, he trimmed the engine down at the same time as he spun the boat around and shoved the shift forward. The boat tipped nose up and plowed the water until it picked up enough speed so that the front dropped down and they skimmed along at forty-five knots.

For the first time in what felt like hours, Tuck breathed. He knew they didn't have long to get ahead. The thugs would find another boat with keys in it or hot-wire one and be on their tail soon. The farther away from the marina they got, the better. Tuck risked flipping the lights on to check the fuel gauge and groaned. Damn, less than a quarter of a tank. That wouldn't get them far.

He'd have to find someplace to ditch the boat and hide or get out and make a run across land. His gaze moved to the woman in the seat beside him.

"Are you two all right?"

"Yes, thank goodness." Julia had thrown back her shawl to check on Lily. The baby snuggled against her mother, her fist bunched in the fabric of Julia's shirt.

A swell of pride filled Tuck's chest at the same time

as an overwhelming fear knotted his gut. "See if you can find life vests for the both of you. They might be under the bench seats." He didn't add that the vests could be necessary in case the boat tipped over or a fast turn threw them both into the lake.

How the hell was he going to keep them safe with men shooting at them? With very little gas to keep the engine going, they couldn't stay on the lake long. Had he chosen the wrong route? Would they have been better off trying to get out by car?

Second-guessing would get him nowhere. They had enough gas to get somewhere. There had to be campgrounds on the lake.

Tuck didn't dare slow down. He held the wheel as steady as he could while Julia moved about the boat, searching the cubbies beneath the seats and locating life vests to fit both Tuck and herself. She even found a small child's vest. Unfortunately it was still far too big to fit Lily.

"Put yours on first," Tuck said.

Julia laid the baby on the backseat while she slipped her arms into her vest and tightened the straps and buckles around her middle. Then she strapped the ill-fitting vest onto Lily, tying it around her snugly enough to keep it from falling off and the baby afloat should they hit the water.

All the while, Tuck kept a watch behind them, not that he could see much. The night sky was filled with millions of stars, but without a full moon, the inky-black lake, churning in the North Dakota wind, revealed nothing.

Until the bad guys caught up with them, Tuck wouldn't be able to see them. By then it would be too late.

Carrying the bundled Lily, Julia moved up to the

seat beside Tuck. "She's not very happy, but it can't be helped." The mother fixed her worried gaze on the baby in her arms, squirming against the straps.

Tuck's chest tightened. He could do nothing more than what he was to make their burden lighter. "Keep a lookout for campgrounds, trailers, tents, RVs. We have to get off the lake soon."

Julia glanced up at him, her forehead dented in a frown. "Why?"

"We don't have enough fuel to outrun them for long."

"Gotcha. I'm looking." Her head swiveled as she peered through the windshield. "You'll have to get closer to the shore for me to see anything."

Tuck struggled with which bank of the river-fed lake to cling to, finally settling on the east side, the boat skimming the surface and the flat North Dakota land stretching into the darkness.

This was only the second time in Tuck's life he'd been scared of anything. The first being less than two months ago during a raid. He, his brother Pierce and Tuck's best friend and fellow FBI agent Mason Carmichael had been assisting the ATF. Tuck had let Mason down, allowing his buddy to walk into a trap by entering the building they suspected contained a militia group's cache of drugs and weapons.

The ensuing explosion had thrown Tuck and Pierce back several yards, knocking the breath out of them and giving them both mild concussions, but keeping them away from the worst of the flames. The ATF team and Mason had died along with the members of the militia inside.

He'd watched as Mason died in Pierce's arms, knowing he could have stopped him from going into that warehouse. His worst fear now was that he would fail Julia and Lily.

He couldn't let that happen.

"There!" Julia pointed to the shore a quarter mile ahead. "What's that?"

As they moved steadily closer, Tuck made out the outline of a playground set complete with swings, slides and teeter-totters. Behind it were neat rows of travel trailers, RVs and tents. A yellow light glowed over a shower building at the center.

He eased the steering wheel to the right, bringing the boat closer to the shore.

Other boats were grounded on the water's edge or anchored a few feet out. Tuck passed the campground.

"Aren't we going to stop and find a car?" Julia asked, her head swiveling, looking behind them.

"Yeah, but we can't pull in too close, or someone will see us." Tuck drove the boat straight for the shore north of the campground.

Julia touched his arm. "Aren't you going to stop? We're going to run aground."

"That's the idea." The bottom of the boat skimmed across sand and gravel, coming to a stop in two feet of water. "You two get out and wait on the shore for me."

Julia shed her vest, gathered her backpack, untied the baby from her life vest and carried her to the front of the boat. When she was ready, she sat on the edge. "What are you going to do?"

"We can't leave the boat here. If the guys chasing us recognize it, they'll know this is where we stopped." He held out his arms for Lily. "Want me to go first and help you two down?"

"No, it's better if I go first, while you hold Lily."

Julia handed the baby girl to Tuck and turned, sliding over the edge into the icy water. As her feet hit bottom, she lost her footing for a second and staggered, arms flailing.

"Careful," Tuck called out, frustrated that he couldn't help, the baby firmly tucked into the crook of his arm.

Julia tipped and fell on her back in the water. She struggled to get her feet under her, the backpack and her shawl weighing her down. Finally, she managed to stand straight, water dripping from every part of her body, her hair hanging like limp ropes in her face.

"Thank goodness you had Lily." Her teeth chattered. "The water is icy cold." She moved closer to the boat, easing her way along the sandy bottom. When she was abreast of the bow, she reached up for Lily.

"Are you sure you're okay?" Tuck held the baby out of her reach.

"Yeah. Wet and cold, but okay."

Tuck handed over the baby.

Julia waded up to the shore and sat on dry ground, holding Lily away from her body to keep the baby away from her cold, wet clothing.

Tuck shook his head, wishing he had gotten out first and helped Julia to shore. But what was done was done. He backed the boat off the gravel, aimed it north and, using the straps of a life vest, tied the steering wheel so that it would stay straight and guide the craft out into the middle of the lake.

Taking a deep breath, Tuck climbed up on the side of the boat, shoved the throttle forward all the way and jumped.

Chapter Five

Julia's heart lodged in her throat and she rose from the ground with Lily in her arms as Tuck hit the water.

He sank to his thighs but remained upright.

Much better landing than Julia's. She shook her head. The chill of the night air left her body trembling.

Tuck waded toward her, reaching out for the baby. "My upper body is dry. Let me have her."

"Thanks. I don't know what happened. One minute I'm standing, the next I'm lying on my back like a turtle in the water." She shrugged off the backpack. "I would have come up sooner if it hadn't been for the backpack." Her eyes widened. "The backpack."

"What?"

"The cell phone is in the backpack." She slipped the straps from her shoulder and laid the bag on dry ground, rifling through the pockets until she surfaced with the device. She pulled it from a pocket filled with chilled lake water, her heart sinking to her knees. "Oh, no."

"It's wet?"

"Soaked." She hit the power key and nothing happened. No lights blinked to life, the screen remained dark and Julia lost all hope of finding the man who'd killed her sister. "It's ruined. How are we going to catch the killer without the video?"

"Let me have it." Tuck held Lily in one arm while he fiddled with the buttons on the phone. When nothing worked, he flipped it over and removed the battery. "Hold this." He handed the phone back to her and dried the battery on his shirt.

While he dried the battery, Julia used his shirt to dry the interior of the phone. Her hands brushed across his skin, warming her in places the cold lake water couldn't touch.

When he handed her the battery, she slipped it into the phone, said a silent prayer and pressed the on button.

Nothing. A shiver shook her so violently she almost dropped the phone.

Tuck's hand closed around hers. "We can't worry about it now. We have to find shelter and get you out of those wet clothes."

"But the video…"

"Can wait." He shoved the phone into his jacket pocket and grabbed the backpack in one hand, still balancing Lily in the other. "Let's go."

Julia scrambled up the bank, running to catch up to Tuck. She slipped the backpack from his hands. "Let me hold this. You've got Lily."

He released the pack and headed toward the campground, his long strides eating the distance.

Tired, cold and aching, it was all Julia could do to keep up. When at last they neared the campers, tents and vehicles, she wondered how they'd convince anyone to help them.

At this time of the early morning, appearing out of nowhere wet and bedraggled, they'd likely scare people to death.

Tuck walked up to a large motor home that stood somewhat isolated, several yards away from the other campers and tents, with the entrance facing away from the campground. He knocked on the door, still holding the baby in his arms.

No answer.

He knocked a little louder, checking behind him to be certain he wasn't seen by the rest of the campground and hadn't made enough noise to stir others from their sleep.

The curtain over the small window in the door shifted to the side and a grizzled older man peered out. "Do you know what time it is?" a muffled voice called out from inside.

Tuck smiled. "Yes, sir. I'm sorry to bother you. I'm Tuck Thunder Horse, FBI. Could you open the door? It's an emergency."

"Show me some proof, and I'll think about it." The old man's gaze swept over Tuck, the bundle in his arms and Julia standing behind him. "I'll warn ya, I have a gun."

"Good. We need help." Tuck pulled his wallet from his back pocket and flipped it open, displaying his FBI card and badge.

Julia shivered. The badge brought back so many memories of her father and her sister. She had to squeeze shut her eyes and swallow hard on the lump rising in her throat to keep from falling apart. She couldn't. Not now. Lily depended on her.

The old man's eyes narrowed. "How do I know those aren't fake?"

"You don't. But I'm carrying a baby, and the woman with me is soaking wet and needs to get dry before hypothermia sets in."

"Oh, for heaven's sake, Marshall, open the door." A woman's voice sounded behind the man.

The curtain fell in place, locks clicked and the door pushed open.

An older woman wearing a faded blue bathrobe, her gray hair poking straight up, waved them in. "Come in, come in. It's getting cold out there. You'll catch your death." She pulled her robe tighter and stepped back, urging her spouse farther into the motor home.

Tuck moved aside to allow Julia to enter first.

"Thank you so much," Julia managed between her chattering teeth.

"Good Lord. Marshall, get the lady a towel. She's freezing."

Marshall grumbled as he squeezed into the tiny bathroom. "Wouldn't need a towel if she stayed out of the lake at night. Only bad things happen to people outside past midnight, I always say."

He returned carrying a fluffy white towel, which he handed over, the grumpy look fading as he took in her pathetic appearance.

"I'm Lois Glimm. This is Marshall, my husband. Now, you two make yourselves at home." Her gaze panned the length of Julia. "I might have a tracksuit that will fit you. Why don't you step into the bathroom and slip out of those wet things?"

"I hate to impose." Another full-body shudder shook her frame, and she smiled and slipped the straps of the backpack off her shoulders. "But, thanks." She hurried into the bathroom and removed the shawl, shirt and jeans, stripping down to her underwear and bra.

The door opened a crack and Lois's hand reached in with a wad of clothing. "Try these, honey."

Julia accepted them and slid the sweatpants up over her legs, the immediate warmth bringing a sigh to her lips. Once she had the sweatshirt pulled down over her body, the shivers abated and she almost felt human. Then she made the mistake of glancing in the mirror. Her hair hung in damp coils around her shoulders, her eyelids were red-rimmed from crying and her face was pale and splotchy. But her wrecked appearance wasn't nearly as upsetting as the reminder that from now on, the only way she'd see this face was in a mirror. She'd never be able to look at her twin again.

Tears welled, filling her eyes. Jillian was dead. Her only sibling was gone. She and Lily were alone in the world with bad guys after them and danger around every corner.

Then she remembered Tuck. He'd saved her more than once thus far. After the initial shock of learning he had a child, he'd stepped up to the plate and batted a thousand, ensuring their safety.

She didn't have time to mourn the loss of her sister. That could wait until the killer was captured and she and Lily were safe.

Carrying her damp clothes wadded in the towel, she stepped out of the bathroom, her shoulders square, her determination firmly in place.

Tuck sat sideways on a towel draped over a leather couch in the surprisingly spacious living area of the motor home with Lily lying on the cushions in front of him. A damp diaper sat folded beside them on the floor.

Tuck had a fresh diaper in one hand and Lily's ankles in the other. He cooed down at her, his dark eyes twinkling.

Lily stared up at the strange man who was her father, her cheeks dimpled in a happy grin.

Tuck slid the diaper beneath her bare bottom and secured the tapes at the sides.

The contents of the backpack had been spread out

on the table beside him, her damp clothing and Lily's lying in a heap.

Julia counted her blessings that she was so anal about her daughter's well-being. She liked to use gallon-size resealable plastic bags to organize her daughter's things. In one she had several diapers. In another she'd placed the powder formula she used to mix milk for Lily. The seals had held, protecting the few diapers and the food needed to see her through the rest of the night and next day.

"Your husband has quite a way with your daughter," Lois remarked. "She's just precious."

Julia shot a glance at Tuck, choosing not to correct the woman's comment about Tuck being her husband. "Thank you."

Lois shook out a plastic grocery bag and stuffed the wet garments into it. "I understand you two were headed to Bismarck by boat when you ran into trouble?"

Again Julia looked to Tuck. What had he told these two kind people?

"That's right," Tuck jumped in. "Got a later start than I'd intended. I think we must have blown a fuse or something. When we got out of the boat, Julia fell in the water. The boat drifted off while I was fishing her out and trying to hold the baby all at once." Tuck lifted Lily in his arms and she turned her face into his shirt, her lips pinching in a sucking motion. He smiled down at her and stroked her cheek with one of his large fingers. "I believe this one is hungry."

"We were pulling up stakes in the morning, headed back to Minneapolis," Lois said. "You could ride with us to Bismarck."

"Are you sure?" Julia asked.

"Absolutely. Fair warning, though…" Lois's lips pressed thin.

Julia frowned, waiting for the clincher.

"We get up early," Marshall said. "We break camp at five so that we can get back home before dark."

"Oh, that's no problem. We're early risers, aren't we, honey?" Julia smiled at Tuck, hugging the fleece sweats around her middle, finally warm inside and out. "Once we get there we can send someone down to find the boat." She reached for one of the empty bottles and held it up. "Do you have potable water I can use to mix the formula for Lily?"

While Lois helped her find bottled water, Julia listened as the men discussed the plan for breaking camp the following morning.

She hoped five o'clock wasn't too late to leave. If the people following them actually stopped at the campground, would they knock on every camper until they found them? Julia prayed they wouldn't.

While Julia fed Lily, Marshall helped Tuck pull out the bed from the fold-out sofa. Lois got sheets and blankets from the closet. Between the two of them, Tuck and Lois had the double bed made in no time.

Julia's pulse kicked into overdrive at the thought of sleeping beside Tuck. The last time she'd shared a bed with the man, she'd ended up pregnant. Not that they'd do anything in the presence of the elderly couple, but the temptation would make things strained between them.

"You and Lily take the bed," Tuck said. "I'll sleep in one of the lounge chairs."

"I could make up a little pallet on the floor for the baby," Lois offered.

"I'd feel better knowing she's close to her mother,"

Tuck protested. "I'll be fine in the lounge chair. Thanks anyway, Mrs. Glimm."

"If you're sure..." Lois looked at Tuck and then the lounge chair.

Tuck was so much bigger than the chair.

Julia bit her tongue, waiting for the Glimms to go to bed before she spoke up. "You two have done so much. Please get some sleep. We're just happy to be warm and dry."

Lois blushed. "Well, then, good night...or what's left of it." She waved Marshall into the back bedroom compartment and closed the door between them.

"Remember..." Marshall called out.

"We know," Tuck said with a grin. "You have a gun."

The generator kicked on, a fan blowing warm air through the motor home, the noise drowning out anything the Glimms might overhear Julia and Tuck saying.

"Take the bed with Lilly," Julia offered. "I'll fit better in the lounge chair."

Tuck shook his head. "I'm not sleeping. But you'd better get some rest. Lily needs it, too." He nodded toward the baby still suckling the nearly empty bottle, eyes closed, her lips moving slowly, stopping and then sucking again.

Julia smoothed the thick black hair from Lily's face and pressed a kiss to her forehead. Her heart ached with the surge of love she always experienced when she stared down at her daughter's sleeping face.

When she glanced up, she caught Tuck looking at her, his dark eyes black and unfathomable.

"You're good with her."

"Thanks. It's easy when I love her so much." She pulled the bottle from the baby's mouth and set it on the end table, laid Lily over her shoulder and patted her back until the baby burped.

Tuck's eyes widened, the corners of his lips lifting momentarily. Then his jaw tightened and his brows furrowed. "Be ready to move if I tell you to."

Julia laid Lily on the bed and turned to Tuck. "You think they'll find us here?"

"I don't think so, but we can't be too careful."

"Right." She set her wet shoes beside the bed, then arranged everything on the table for quick packing as soon as Tuck gave her the word. All the while she moved around the cramped living space, she found herself bumping into Tuck every step of the way. Each time, her heart leaped and her breath caught in her chest.

The same attraction she'd had a year ago hadn't dampened one bit. And that scared the hell out of her.

When she'd finally done all she could to prepare, she lay down beside Lily, facing the lounge chair Tuck had stretched out in. He lay back with his arm behind his head, his gaze on Lily. "She's beautiful," he whispered, his lips turning up at the corners.

Julia smiled, her hand reaching out to pull the blanket up around their daughter. "She looks just like her father."

The smile disappeared, his jaw hardening into stone. "You should have told me."

A fist squeezed Julia's heart. "I know." She turned away from the look of accusation in Tuck's eyes. She couldn't undo what was done. If she could, she'd bring her sister back and tell Tuck he was going to be a father as soon as she'd learned the truth.

But she couldn't. A tear slipped from the corner of her eye and trickled across her cheek.

No matter the mistakes you made, life went on.

For some.

She squeezed shut her eyes, willing away the rush of tears pushing up into her throat. Images of Jillian when they were camping with both parents flooded into her mind. Her mother pinning on Jillian's badge when she'd graduated from Quantico. Jillian holding her hand through labor and delivery when Lily came into the world, kicking and bawling her lungs out. Julia couldn't conceive of life without her sister there.

The tears fell in earnest. Julia fought to contain her sobs, to keep the noise down so that she didn't disturb the Glimms and so that Tuck wouldn't know she'd given in to grief.

The edge of the bed dipped. Warm, strong arms lifted her from the pillow and pulled her against a solid wall of muscle.

She stared at the blue button-down, the texture of the fabric swimming in the wash of tears. Her fingers curled into cotton and she cried.

Tuck spoke softly, his words making no sense to her grieving mind. It sounded as if he spoke in the native tongue of the Lakota people. His hands brushed the hair from her damp cheeks and stroked down her back.

Before long, her tears ceased and her senses warmed with awareness of the man holding her in his arms. Her fingers slipped beneath his shirt, resting against his taut skin, reveling in the heat of his body. She couldn't get close enough. The chill of her sadness and loss made her body tremble.

He gathered her closer, his hands sliding beneath her sweatshirt, his calloused fingers caressing her skin, tracing a line from the base of her spine up her back.

Her breath hitched, her blood zinging through her veins, pooling at her core.

Tuck Thunder Horse hadn't changed, and Julia's reaction to him was no less intense. She wanted him desperately, craved the pleasure of his touch to wash away the ache that filled her, body and soul.

But she couldn't give him her heart. Not as long as he was with the FBI. The bureau had taken her parents from her, and now that she'd lost her sister as well, the dangers of an FBI agent's life scared her even more. She couldn't give him her heart only for it to be broken by his ultimate death.

"No." She shoved against his chest, pushing him away. "We shouldn't."

His hands froze on her back, his body going rigid. For a long moment he sat still, then he rose from the bed and stared down at her. "You're right. We shouldn't. You made your position very clear nearly a year ago when you couriered over the annulment papers. I can respect that. I won't misunderstand you again." He turned away and stood at a window, pulling the slat of the blind down to peer out.

Julia dragged the blanket up around her chin. With Tuck's body warmth gone, she shivered, her body shaking from more than just the cold.

She longed to tell him to come back to bed—she literally had to bite her tongue to keep from calling out to him. That made her realize with dread that she could fall in love with Tuck just as quickly and easily as she had the first time they'd met.

And she couldn't. Her heart couldn't handle another loss.

Chapter Six

Tuck stood guard over Lily and Julia throughout the remainder of the night, watching out the window for any sign of the goons who'd chased them down to the marina. From the motor home's position in the campground, Tuck couldn't see to the lake's edge. All he could do was hope the boat he and Julia had abandoned had traveled a lot farther north before running aground.

When Julia finally fell into a troubled sleep, Tuck alternated between looking out the window and studying his daughter and the woman he'd married.

Lily lay curled against Julia, her tiny fist clenched around her mother's hair.

Julia spooned the baby with her body. Even in her sleep, the mother was careful not to roll over and smother the child. Her hand rested on Lily's hip, as if to keep her within reach.

They were as different as night and day. One pale-skinned and blonde, the other dark-haired with the hint of darkening skin tones.

Tuck's heart squeezed in his chest. Lily was his daughter. One day she'd call him Daddy. How could one tiny being take him to his knees so quickly?

He reached out and stroked her cheek, the softness bringing home to him how defenseless she was. She couldn't take care of herself. With thugs after them, Julia could continue to run but for how long before they finally caught up to her? Lily would be caught in the cross fire. Collateral damage.

Tuck's gut wrenched at the thought of anyone harming the defenseless child or her mother, neither of whom had done anything to deserve the attack. But until the killer was caught, they'd remain in danger.

Several times during the early-morning hours, Tuck checked the waterlogged cell phone, hoping it would miraculously restart, only to be disappointed each time. He'd have to get it to Skeeter, the techie at the Minneapolis office. He had all the equipment and skill necessary to extract the data. Hopefully, once he'd downloaded the clip, he could sharpen the image enough to identify the murderer. Then it was only a matter of catching him. Easier said than done when the killer faced life in prison.

Before dawn, an alarm buzzed in the back compartment. Tuck nudged Julia. "Time to get up."

She jerked to an upright position, her eyes wide. "Did they find us?"

"No. It's five o'clock. We leave in less than half an hour."

Several minutes later, the Glimms emerged from the bedroom, hair combed and dressed for a day on the road.

Tuck sluiced water over his face in the tiny bathroom and scrubbed his teeth with a spare toothbrush the Glimms gave him. When he emerged, he still felt tired, but all traces of sleepiness had been washed away. He needed to be on top of his game in case anything happened on their way to Bismarck.

While Julia used the facilities, Lois held Lily.

The two men folded the bed into the couch and set the living area to rights, then stepped outside to bring the sliding panels in on the sides of the motor home.

Tuck insisted Julia remain inside. Summer in North Dakota meant early daylight and late sunsets. Not long after they got up, the sun had risen over the horizon and people in the other campsites began to stir. Tuck didn't want her seen by anyone in the campground.

Once the automated jacks had been lifted and everything was stowed, they were ready.

Lois insisted on Tuck sitting in the front with Marshall so they could have "man talk" while she and Julia sat in the living area that had shrunk to nearly half its size with the closing of the sliding panels.

As they headed north on a farm-to-market road, Tuck kept a vigilant watch out for other vehicles. Most of what they passed were farm trucks or SUVs with weathered farmers, heading to or from Bismarck for supplies or groceries.

With the engine noise from the diesel engine, Tuck couldn't hear the conversation behind him. The flipside was they couldn't hear what he and Marshall were saying.

"You know I didn't buy the story about you two traveling by boat."

"I figured as much." Tuck hadn't wanted to tell the Glimms the whole story for fear they'd want to call in the cops and place Julia and Lily in jeopardy. If Jillian hadn't instructed her sister not to call in the police, he'd have gone to his buddy Josh immediately. As it was, Tuck didn't trust anyone but himself with the lives of his daughter and her mother. "Suffice it to say, we ran into some trouble farther south and had to leave the only way we could."

"Did you kill someone?" Marshall shot a narrow-eyed glance Tuck's way.

"No, but two people died who shouldn't have. I didn't want the next two to be Julia and Lily."

Marshall nodded. For a long time he didn't speak.

The closer they drove toward Bismarck, the more tense Tuck got, his hand gripping his cell phone so hard his knuckles turned white.

When they came within reception range, he hesitated, his finger ready to speed-dial the FBI satellite office. At the last minute, he changed his mind. "Could you drop us off at a car-rental place near the airport?"

Marshall nodded. "I can spot you the rental. If you're trying to lay low, you won't want your own credit cards showing up anywhere."

Tuck stared across at the old man. "You'd trust me not to take advantage of you? You don't even know us."

"I consider myself a good judge of character." He shrugged, glancing in the rearview mirror into the back of the motor home at his wife. "Gotta say this is the most excitement I've had on one of these trips." He nodded at the mirror. "And Lois is happy with the baby, seeing as our own kids haven't given us a single grandchild yet." He shrugged. "Consider it just doing my part."

"Thanks. I'd appreciate it if you didn't mention our stay with you to anyone until we get this mess figured out."

"I promise, but getting her to keep her mouth shut might be an issue." Marshall jerked his head toward the rear where his wife sat holding Lily. "Good luck." His lips quirked up. "She means well, but she doesn't know a stranger, and sometimes that can lead to interesting situations."

Tuck grinned. "Like us?"

Marshall chuckled. "Like you."

They entered Bismarck from the south, passing the airport. At the first rental-car agency, Marshall pulled in and parked. "Stay here," he said.

A few minutes later, he emerged with a sheaf of papers and a key. He immediately disappeared into a parking lot.

Tuck kept a sharp lookout for anyone who looked even remotely suspicious.

"What's the plan?" Julia moved to the front of the motor home, hovering behind the seats.

"Stay in the shadows. We can't risk you being seen." Tuck whispered so that Lois wouldn't hear. "You need to put your hair up under something."

"I have a baseball cap that I use when I go fishing with Marshall. Let me get it." Lois handed the baby to Julia and went to the bedroom, where she rooted through several closets and drawers.

Julia smiled. "Lois wears a hearing aid. She could hear your entire conversation."

Tuck's lips pressed together. "I hope she won't say anything."

"Not to worry." Lois appeared carrying a green, white and black Fighting Sioux baseball cap. "I won't mention a word of it to anyone. Even to Marshall for that comment on my not being able to keep my mouth shut."

Julia snorted. "See?"

Mrs. Glimm pressed a finger to her lips. "Let that be our little secret. Marshall thinks I'm still hard of hearing—it's a good way for me to hear all the things he thinks I shouldn't know about. Let me hold Lily while you put your hair up." She took the baby from Julia, her face softening with a smile. "You have to contact us—when you can safely." She glanced up, her brows knitting. "I do hope you all will be okay. Dreadful thing, losing your sister like that." The older woman's gaze dropped to the baby. "You take care of this little one and bring her to see me someday."

Julia twisted her thick, long blond hair in a braid and wound it around her head, holding it in place while she slipped the cap over it.

Even though it had been his idea, he hated to see that beautiful hair tucked away. After an entire year, Tuck still hadn't forgotten how good it felt to run his hands through the silken strands.

Even with the tresses hidden, she couldn't disguise her beauty. Blue eyes shone through thick lashes, her skin was as pale as porcelain and lush dusty-rose lips begged to be kissed.

A fist-size knot formed in Tuck's belly. She'd left him the day after their impulsive wedding. Served him papers through an impersonal messenger and then withheld the information about something as important as the birth of their daughter.

Why?

Julia didn't strike him as flighty. Granted, what they'd done had been impetuous, but was it enough of a reason to skip out on him, leaving only a scribbled note? He frowned. She'd refused to see him when he'd tried to contact her. What had made her run?

Tuck turned away, unable to look at Julia without thinking about that night they'd spent together, lying naked in the king-size bed of the casino's hotel room.

A dark gray sedan pulled up next to the motor home and stopped. Marshall Glimm climbed out and entered the motor home through the side door.

"Here's the keys, the paperwork in case you get

stopped and some cash." He handed Tuck the rental agreement, keys and a couple of hundred-dollar bills.

Tuck held up his hands. "I can't take your money. I wouldn't take the rental if I could get it myself without a credit card." He took the keys and the paperwork, noting the Glimms' home address. "I'll be sure to reimburse you for the rental as soon as we're safe." Tuck turned to Julia. "Ready?"

She nodded, taking the baby from Lois. "Ready."

"Wait." Marshall hurried into the bedroom and returned carrying a hard plastic case. He set it on the sofa and flipped open the catches.

Inside, nestled on velvet-covered foam, lay an antique pistol the likes of which Tuck had seen only in magazines.

"Told you I had a gun." The old man puffed out his chest.

"Oh, Marshall, that's not a gun. That's an antique." Lois waved her hand at the weapon.

Marshall's brows drew together above his nose. "It works, and I have the ammunition that goes with it." He opened a compartment in the case, revealing bright silver bullets. "It's a Colt revolver, thirty caliber with a nickel finish and pearl handgrips."

"Can I?" Tuck couldn't resist. He lifted the weapon from the case and balanced it in his hand. The cool metal and sleek grips fit his palm perfectly. "Nice." He laid the antique in the case.

"I want you to have it," Marshall said.

Lois snorted. "Whatever for?"

Her husband's brows drew together. "Protection."

"From what?" Lois laughed. "Jesse James and Billy the Kid?"

Tuck smiled. "I appreciate the thought, but I can't take it."

"You need protection. I'd offer you something more up-to-date, but my nine-millimeter is locked up in my gun safe back home in Minneapolis."

"We'll manage without. Thanks anyway." Tuck grabbed the backpack that had been repacked with the damp clothing and slung it over one shoulder. "Thank you for helping us. I promise we'll be in touch soon."

Julia hugged Lois and surprised Marshall by hugging him, too. "You have been wonderful. I'll call as soon as it's safe."

Lois sighed, brushing a hand across an errant tear. "Take care."

Tuck dropped down the steps, looked left and right. When he determined the coast was clear, he opened the car door and motioned for Julia.

With Lily settled in the sling and snuggled close to her body beneath the still-damp shawl, Julia descended the steps, her green baseball cap pulled down low over her face.

She slid into the passenger seat of the rental car and pulled the visor down, blocking light from revealing too much of the interior.

Tuck sat behind the steering wheel, closed the door and sketched a salute to the Glimms. Without wasting too much time, he pulled out of the parking lot and headed north into Bismarck, forming a plan as he went.

JULIA BUCKLED HER SEAT BELT and sat quietly beside Tuck, a hard ball of sadness settled in her gut. Lois and Marshall were just the kind of folks who made wonderful grandparents. Julia wondered what Tuck's mother was like. Would she play with Lily and rock her to sleep?

Would his siblings acknowledge the baby's existence and want her to be a part of their lives?

A lump lodged in Julia's throat. Not only would Lily never meet her maternal grandparents, she'd never remember her aunt Jillian, who'd doted on her from the day she was born.

A tear slid down the cheek closest to the window. Julia discreetly reached up and brushed it away. Tuck didn't need to deal with a fragile woman, not when his daughter's life was at stake. There would be time to mourn later, when they recovered and deciphered the video and the killer had been brought to justice.

The enormity of what they had to do while staying out of sight threatened to overwhelm her. "Where are we going?"

"We need to find a place to stay until I can figure out how to get the cell phone to the experts."

"A teacher friend of mine lives in Bismarck. Could we stay there?"

"No. The killer knows who you are, and by now he knows you're with me. If there is a rogue police officer or FBI agent, he'll know how to track us through our contacts. We have to stay beneath the radar. No digital or electronic communication with friends or family, and no use of credit cards."

"I only have about twenty dollars in cash." Julia looked up at him. "I'm going to need diapers and formula for Lily before the end of the day, and those aren't cheap. And to keep her safe and the police from pulling us over, we'll need to invest in an infant car seat."

"I have enough cash to get by for the day, but it won't go very far." He checked his watch. "First thing is to get you and Lily somewhere safe."

He drove to the edge of town to a dingy street with

an old hotel whose faded sign read VACANCY in red neon lights. Parking the car behind a large trash bin, out of sight of the road, Tuck turned to her. "Stay here. I'll be right back."

Julia didn't remind him that she didn't have anywhere else to go. Instead, she just nodded.

Tuck left.

Lily stirred in the sling, her mouth working in a sucking motion. Thankfully, Mrs. Glimm had insisted on Julia taking two extra bottles of water with her. Laying the baby on the seat beside her, she combined the formula and the water in a baby bottle and shook it until it mixed thoroughly.

Gathering Lily in her arms, she popped the bottle in her mouth. The sun had been up for a couple of hours, but it was still early morning in Bismarck. The steady hum of morning rush-hour traffic built with each passing minute on the nearby highway.

An unkempt man wearing dirty jeans and an equally filthy jacket pushed a shopping cart laden with blankets, plastic bags and junk through the parking lot. He passed by the car where Julia waited.

The man bent and peered into window. When he spotted Julia, he held out his hand. "Haven't had breakfast in two days."

Julia leaned away from the window, recoiling from his filth at the same time her heart went out to the obviously homeless man. She reached into her backpack for her wallet and emptied the change into her palm. Then she turned the key in the ignition enough to engage the electric windows and rolled the passenger window down enough to hand the money through. Balancing the baby and bottle in one hand, she held out the other with the change in it.

The man grabbed her wrist.

Julia yelped, releasing her hold on the coins. With Lily curled into her other arm, she couldn't leverage herself out of the bum's grip. "Let go!"

"I'm hungry. I need more than that." He yanked on her arm, nearly pulling her through the window.

The bottle fell from Lily's mouth. Her face scrunched into an angry scowl and she screamed with all the lung power of a four-month-old.

Afraid to draw any more attention to the car behind the trash bin than she already had, Julia adjusted her position and fought back.

The man's grip was much stronger and he had the advantage of his position standing over her. He bent her arm over the lip of the window, the beveled glass pressing into her skin.

Pain shot through her wrist and forearm. If he pushed much harder, the bone would snap.

"Let go," Julia said between gritted teeth.

The man reached his other hand into the window, groping for the door handle.

Afraid of what he'd do if he got the door open, Julia waited until his attention was fully on getting the door open, then she jerked her hand loose of his grip and jammed the heel of her palm into the man's nose.

The bum staggered backward, his hands rising to cover his nose, blood running over his fingers.

Julia punched the button on the door, and the window inched upward.

The bum's eyes rounded, his bloody lips curling back in a sneer. Then he charged the car, slamming his hands against the glass. He left bloody handprints on the glass and reared back to hit again.

Julia braced herself, certain the glass would shatter and the bum would be inside, tearing her and Lily apart.

The dirty man charged, but before his body rammed into the car, he was jerked around and thrown to the ground, where he lay moaning.

"Unlock the door," Tuck said as he jogged around to the driver's side.

Her heart pounding, Julia hit the unlock button, her gaze on the man pushing to his knees. *Hurry, Tuck.*

Tuck slid behind the steering wheel, cranked the engine and backed out of the parking lot. Julia's attacker staggered toward them.

Once out in the street, Tuck floored the accelerator and they shot away from the dingy motel.

Julia clutched Lily to her chest, plugging the bottle back in her mouth.

The baby stopped crying immediately, her fingers curling around the bottle.

Leaning back against her seat, Julia willed her pulse to slow. Her entire body shook with the aftershock of being attacked. "I'm sorry. He just looked so pathetic."

"That's okay. We weren't going to stay there anyway."

"Why?"

"The place was a pig's sty, the clerk was high and they rented by the hour."

Julia's eyes widened. "Oh."

While Tuck searched for another hotel, Julia sat quietly, wondering if this nightmare would ever end. It seemed only to be getting worse.

Within fifteen minutes, Tuck found another hotel. Still off the beaten path, it was small and older, but the exterior was freshly painted and the owner was an older couple trying to sell the place as a bed-and-breakfast.

Julia sat in the car, hugging Lily close, on alert for anyone who looked even remotely like trouble. Now she almost wished she had the antique gun Marshall had offered. If not to use, then to brandish wildly as a threat to anyone who might come near, and to hell with keeping a low profile.

Shortly after he'd left her, Tuck returned carrying a key. He climbed into the car, pulled it around to the back of the building and parked near a large bush.

"Now what?" Julia asked.

"Now you get some rest while I see what I can do about the video on the cell phone."

She touched his arm. "You aren't going to the FBI with it, are you?"

He stared at her hand. "If you mean, am I going to the office with it, then no."

Julia frowned. "Then what *do* you mean?"

"My brother is due in today from Quantico. He's also a member of the FBI. I'm going to contact him."

"If they know you're with me, don't you think they'll be watching him to see if you try to make contact?"

Tuck nodded. "I'd already thought of that. I'll make sure I'm not seen."

"Lily and I are supposed to wait here until you return?"

"Can you think of anything else you could be doing in a town the size of Bismarck? It might be bigger than Fort Yates, but it's not big enough for you to go out in public and risk your life and Lily's."

Julia's shoulders slumped. What she really wanted to say was that she didn't want him to leave her. But that would make her look needy and helpless. Tuck was only trying to resolve the case as soon as possible. "When does your brother get in?"

"In four hours. I could use some sleep, and if I'm not mistaken, so could you." He glanced down at Lily. "Any chances she'll nap for long?"

Julia smiled. "Lily naps off and on all day. She just finished a bottle, so she's good for a couple of hours at least."

"Then let's go. I don't know what the day has in store for us, but I'd feel better knowing we were both rested."

Tuck exited the vehicle and came around to hold the door for her.

Julia gathered Lily and the backpack and, heart pounding, stepped out of the car, her gaze shooting in all directions, punchy from having been chased, shot at and nearly yanked through a car window. Even though the last incident had nothing to do with the men who were after her, it had been enough to leave her shaky and scared. She didn't know how much more danger she'd be able to handle.

A dark shadow darted out from beneath a bush and raced across the parking lot.

Julia yelped and flung herself toward Tuck.

His arms wrapped around her and the baby. He held her until she steadied, a warm chuckle rumbling through his chest.

"W-what was that?" she asked.

He nodded toward the rear of the rental car. "Check it out."

Beneath the back bumper, a black cat sat, calmly cleaning its paws.

Julia laughed, the sound coming out more of a choked sob than anything, and she leaned her head against Tuck's chest. "Why is this happening?"

"*Wakantanka* has his plan."

"*Wakantanka?*"

"The Great Spirit." Tuck smiled down at her, his finger brushing across Lily's cheek then rising to dash away an errant tear trailing down Julia's face. "It is the will of *Wakantanka*."

Anger bubbled up inside Julia. "Was it the will of the Great Spirit to take my sister from me?" She pulled away from Tuck and straightened, her eyes filling with tears she refused to let fall. "I'm sorry, I shouldn't have said that. *Wakantanka* didn't kill my sister. Probably the same man I saw killing the NIGC representative killed her—the one in the video that we can't access anymore."

Tuck nodded, his face carved out of stone. "We need to take this conversation into the motel room."

Her heart bumping against her chest, Julia glanced around, checking for killers, bums or others bent on making her life a living hell. Tuck was right. They needed to get out of the open to somewhere they could keep Lily safe.

Tuck hooked his hand through Julia's elbow and ushered her toward the last room on the very end of the hotel. Once inside with the door closed behind them, Julia met her next hurdle of the day.

One queen-size bed filled the tiny room with barely enough of a gap on each side for a grown person to walk. With no other lounge chair, sofa or floor space, she'd be forced to share the bed with Tuck and Lily.

A shiver of awareness rippled across her skin.

How would she sleep with him lying so closely? She'd barely gotten any sleep early that morning, too aware of every move Tuck made. She'd watched him from beneath her lashes as he moved around the inside of the motor home, his broad shoulders stretching the fabric of his T-shirt, the muscles beneath rippling. Exhausted, she'd finally drifted off, before the Glimms' alarm had buzzed.

Now alone with Tuck with a bed in front of them, Julia's breath quickened, her blood zinging through her system, hot, thick and aroused.

Lily squirmed in her arms, a living, breathing reminder of the reality of their situation.

With a small child between them, she'd have nothing to worry about. Passion couldn't run rampant; lust couldn't spin out of control as it had the night they'd met.

Lily was the reason she'd gone to Tuck in the first place. This baby was her world, her reason for living. She'd protect her no matter what. Love and passion had no place in their current circumstances.

Then why did her body burn with need? And why did she want Tuck to wrap her in his arms and make sweet love to her until all the bad dreams went away?

Chapter Seven

Tuck set an alarm on his phone for an hour before his brother Pierce's plane was due to land in Bismarck. Although he was a fellow FBI agent, Pierce was perhaps the only person he could trust in the city. In spite of whatever corruption had led Jillian to distrust law enforcement, Tuck knew his brother would never let him down. The sooner he got the cell phone to him, the sooner they could get it analyzed and see if they could retrieve the video stored on its waterlogged chip.

After checking out the window one last time, Tuck lay on the bed on the other side of Lily, away from Julia.

The scent of Julia's shampoo mingled with that of baby powder and formula, tugging at Tuck's heart, making him long for something that just wouldn't happen.

Julia had dumped him and moved on, denying him knowledge of his baby.

Tuck's teeth ground together. He wouldn't let Julia keep the child from him any longer. Lily had a right to know her father and the Thunder Horse heritage. She belonged with him just as much as she belonged with her mother.

Forcing his eyes closed, he blocked out the sound of their breathing, concentrating on the noises outside the motel until even those faded and he drifted into an exhausted sleep, where he dreamed of bad guys stealing his daughter, of a heartbroken Julia staring at him with those soulful blue eyes, begging him to find her.

The alarm on his cell phone jerked him out of the dream. He sat up, breathing hard, his heart thundering. With only an hour to spare, he had to position himself to intercept Pierce without drawing the attention of anyone on the lookout for him.

He had turned off the wireless on his phone when he'd arrived in Bismarck, afraid the GPS capability would allow anyone with access to his number to pinpoint his location.

Cut off from his office and having skipped out on his partner in Fort Yates, Tuck knew he was treading on dangerous ground, making his actions suspect, even to the good guys.

Julia stirred, her eyes blinking open. "Is it time?" she whispered, her glance skimming across the sleeping baby before moving to him.

"Yes."

She sat up, rubbing the sleep from her eyes. With a deep sigh, she grabbed the pen and pad of paper from the nightstand and scribbled something down before handing the top sheet to him. "Those are the things we'll need for Lily."

Tuck stared down at the list that included diapers, formula and a car seat. "What about you?" He reached for the tablet and ripped off another sheet of paper, stuffing it and the pen into his pocket.

"I'm not worried about me. Just take care of her needs when you can. I'll survive with what we have."

He tucked the list into the same pocket as the pen. "You know what to do?"

She nodded. "Don't go outside this room. Don't

answer the door unless it's you and don't answer the phone." With a smile, she added. "How'd I do?"

Tuck smiled down at her, a swell of pride and something else filling his chest. "You'd make a good special agent."

Her smile slipped from her face and her gaze shifted to her sleeping baby. "That's not something I've ever wanted."

Wanting to pursue her murmured statement, but out of time, Tuck leaned down and pressed a kiss to Lily's cheek. Julia sat so close that, on impulse, Tuck brushed a kiss across her forehead. "Be careful. I'll be back as soon as I can."

Julia stood, her hand snagging his jacket. "Tuck?"

He paused, his gaze taking in the worried frown.

"Be careful yourself." She stood on her toes and kissed him, her lips lightly skimming his.

The instant she touched him, shocks of awareness blitzed throughout his system. Tuck's arm circled her waist and he pulled her closer, deepening the kiss, adrenaline and desire pulsing through his veins when she didn't push him away.

When he set her away from him, she ran her tongue across her bottom lip, her eyes glazed, her hands falling to her sides. She opened her mouth to speak.

Tuck didn't wait for her to say the kiss had been a mistake, that it couldn't happen again. Before she could steal the magic out of what had just happened between them, he turned and strode out of the tiny room, closing the door between them.

Tuck climbed into the car and drove south toward the airport, his mind on the task ahead, his heart in the motel behind him. If he didn't focus, he'd blow this gig, risking his life, and Julia's and Lily's.

At the first convenience store, he stopped and purchased a prepaid cell phone, a pair of sunglasses, a gray baseball cap and a heather-gray North Dakota sweatshirt. In the car, he shrugged out of his leather jacket and slipped the sweatshirt over his head. With the ball cap and the sunglasses, he looked like anybody else in Bismarck.

At the airport, he parked in the short-term parking and waited in his car until a minivan full of people pulled up close to him. When five people, ranging in age from teens to adults, got out, he trailed their group, slipping into the airport as if he was one of the family.

Once inside, Tuck entered the souvenir shop and purchased a black sweatshirt and a black baseball cap. He regretted spending so much of his cash when he didn't have a way to replenish his limited supply, but given the seriousness of the situation, he didn't want to gain a tail and lead him back to Julia and Lily.

He checked the Arrivals digital display board. Pierce's plane had just landed. It would be only a few minutes before the older Thunder Horse brother strode through the exit. If Tuck wanted to catch him and remain anonymous, he'd have to do it on Pierce's way out of the airport when a mob of people exited the building at once.

Ducking into the men's restroom, he entered a stall and closed the door. Quickly, he tugged the black sweatshirt over the gray one, jammed the green hat in his waistband beneath his shirt and pulled the black hat over his head. Sunglasses shading his eyes, he pulled the pen and crumpled piece of blank paper from his pocket, scribbled a note to Pierce and wadded it up like a piece of trash.

Footsteps sounded on the tiles near the sinks. Tuck

peered through the gap between the door and the stall walls. Two men in black trousers and black leather jackets stood at the sink. One pressed a cell phone to his ear. Both wore sunglasses, and one had a tattoo on his neck.

His heart thumping like a bass drum, Tuck forced himself to remain silent, backing up to the rear of the stall, his feet as far out of view as possible.

While one man stood guard at the exit, the other man on the cell phone grunted, "Yeah. Will do." He pocketed the cell phone and joined the guy at the exit.

Tuck held his breath, counting the seconds. If these two were watching for Pierce, he'd have very little wiggle room to get a message to his brother and escape without being noticed. "Too many people. Let's wait near the exit."

Footsteps announced their departure.

Tuck counted to ten and emerged from the bathroom. People wheeling carry-on bags headed his way from the gates.

When Pierce appeared in the crowd, Tuck slipped from the bathroom several people ahead of his brother. He walked slower than Pierce, timing it so that his brother would come abreast of him as they passed through the exit doors.

The two thugs who'd been in the bathroom stood at the exit, conspicuously panning the wave of passengers and family members leaving the building.

Tuck ducked between a man and his wife as he neared the men in black, smiled and said something, slowing their progress.

Pierce caught up and waited for the threesome to continue. As all four of them walked through the door, Tuck let the couple move ahead. Purposely bumping into Pierce, he muttered in a low voice, *"Wakantanka yuha yuwakape miye,"* meaning "The Great Spirit has blessed me."

He slipped the paper into Pierce's empty hand and pushed ahead of him, ducking in behind a large family of Native Americans parading their returning relative toward a van in the parking lot.

He didn't look back, keeping a furtive eye out of his peripheral vision for anyone who might have witnessed the exchange.

When he reached the rental car, he jumped in. Forcing himself to remain calm, he glanced back at the terminal building.

He watched Pierce pull his keys from his pocket as he headed for the long-term parking lot. The note had disappeared, his fist closed tightly around the key fob.

The two men dressed in black pants and black leather jackets followed at a distance. Any other time, Tuck might not have noticed them. But the way they watched Pierce and the fact that neither carried a bag, suitcase or briefcase sent up a red flag. They stopped on the curb, hands tucked in their pockets.

Tuck remained parked in the short-term parking lot, ducked low in the driver's seat until Pierce climbed into his truck and drove through the tollbooth.

The two men at the terminal curb bolted for a dark sedan beside them, climbed in and shot forward, sliding into traffic a couple of cars behind Pierce.

Tuck swore.

He exited the parking lot slowly, allowing Pierce to take a long lead with the dark sedan tailing him. He couldn't follow his brother in case the guys pursuing Pierce noticed. He had to trust his brother to read the note, lose the sedan and meet him at the designated department store in the baby-supplies section.

Tuck took the short route, zipping around the airport, keeping an eye out behind him for anyone following. So far, so good. He cruised down several residential streets to make certain, driving slowly to allow anyone following him to catch up.

When he was convinced the coast was clear, he continued on the most direct route to the store, parking in the crowd of vehicles that filled the parking area.

After a quick look around, he entered the store, grabbed a shopping cart and, with the list Julia had given him, raced through the food section for items that didn't need refrigeration or a can opener. He didn't get much, knowing they couldn't weigh themselves down if they had to leave the motel in a hurry.

Then he headed for the baby section. If Pierce had read the note and hadn't had any trouble losing the followers, he'd be there in the next two or three minutes.

When Tuck stepped into the row with the diapers, he compared the list to the endless selection of brands and sizes and groaned.

"Not your size?" a voice sounded behind him.

Tuck spun, his heart bouncing into his throat.

When he spotted his brother, he let go of the breath he'd been holding and pulled Pierce into a bear hug.

"Easy, now. I saw you yesterday in D.C., remember?" Pierce pulled back, frowning. "I hear you're in trouble."

Tuck closed his eyes and pinched the bridge of his nose. "I need to find this type and size of diapers, and I haven't got a clue."

Pierce glanced at the list and then at the rows of diapers. "What happened at Fort Yates?"

Tuck pulled the cap from his head and ran his fingers through his hair. "You're not going to believe this."

"Try me."

"I thought my wife had been killed, but it turns out that it was my wife's twin sister who was murdered, and my wife is the only witness to who might have done it. We have a videotape of the killer that we can't access, and since he knows we've got it, she and I are on the run with our baby." Tuck slipped the cap back on his head and shrugged. "That's it, in a nutshell."

Pierce blinked, but other than that small eye movement, he didn't show any other signs of the shock Tuck felt over the startling events of the past twenty-four hours. "Want to run that by me again a little slower and maybe sprinkle in a few more details?"

Tuck pulled him aside as a young mother wheeled by, an infant strapped in a molded plastic carrier in the cart. When she'd moved on to another aisle, Tuck quickly told Pierce the story, whispering low enough no one else could hear.

When he'd finished, Pierce whistled softly. "Got a problem, don't you?" He grinned. "And a wife and kid? Really? I'm an uncle? How'd that happen?"

"Ex-wife, and that story can wait until later." Tuck glanced around, his heart swelling several times larger at the sound of Pierce declaring himself an uncle. So much had happened, he still hadn't completely wrapped his arms around his new status as a father.

"Mom will be beside herself. You sneaky dog, you." Pierce clapped a hand to Tuck's back before his teasing mood faded, his face growing serious. "I spoke to Behling this morning before I boarded in D.C. and again at my layover in Minneapolis. The unit is in an uproar. Someone is spreading the rumor that you're missing because you're aiding the person who murdered the NIGC agent and the girl, saying you paid this person to kill them both."

"What?" Tuck staggered back. "What motivation would I have to kill an NIGC rep or Julia's sister?"

"No one has made the connection yet that the dead woman is not the schoolteacher they think she is." Pierce shrugged. "They figure you're on the run because you're guilty of something. Give folks enough time and they'll think you and the NIGC commissioner were cooking books."

"The only thing I'm guilty of is falling for the wrong girl and getting her pregnant over a year ago. The rest is fiction. No one's believing all that garbage, are they?"

"Not in *our* office, but Josh had a hard time explaining to the boss why you went missing."

"I couldn't contact him. Julia's sister said to trust no one, especially not the FBI."

Pierce grinned. "You're trusting me."

"We're family."

"The Sioux County sheriff wants you for questioning. Until you come forward, all anyone can do is speculate—and you know how wild that can get."

Tuck sucked in a deep breath in an attempt to relax the tension from his shoulders. He didn't have time to worry about the rumors flying around the bureau and the Sioux County sheriff's office. "Help me find these things. I have to get back to Julia and the baby." He pushed the list toward Pierce.

Pierce held up his hands, refusing to take the list. "I don't know anything about babies. You keep it. You're the father. In the meantime, give me the busted cell phone. I'll make sure it gets to someone who can work magic and retrieve the video."

Tuck stared into his brother's eyes as he handed off the damaged cell phone. "This is the only hard evidence we have of who killed the NIGC rep. Julia's sister was adamant about her not going to the police with it, and specifically said not to trust the FBI, which leads me to believe we could have some bad blood running through the bureau."

"I understand. And how would Julia's sister know that?"

"I don't know, but it's hard not to trust the words of a dying woman."

"Gotcha. I'll be extra careful."

"Pierce, you know that with the cell phone in your hands, you've now become a target."

"I can handle it." Pierce slipped the device into his pocket and laid a hand on his brother's shoulder. "Question is, can you? You've got two other souls to protect."

"I'm doing the best I can. If we lose the data stored in the memory, the only other option we have is for Julia to try to identify the killer. She witnessed it at the same time her sister recorded the event."

Pierce whistled. "She might as well paint a great big bull's-eye on her chest. Whoever killed the NIGC dude will be hot on her trail, wanting to erase any memory one way or another."

Exactly Tuck's estimation of the case. "They've already shot at us. We know they aren't playing with toy guns."

"Are you sure you don't want to let the boss in on this?"

"It's best I don't get anywhere close to the office until this thing settles and we find out who is responsible. After what happened at the Stanton warehouse two months ago, I can't risk our supervisor pulling me off the case and sending me back to Quantico for additional decompression training."

Pierce's lips thinned to a straight, tight line. Having

just returned from the same training as Tuck, Pierce shook his head.

He'd had more to lose than even Tuck. Tuck had lost his best friend to the explosion. Pierce had lost a friend, and in the aftermath, he'd lost his fiancée, as well.

Mason's sister Roxanne had been less than understanding that Pierce and Tuck had survived and her brother had been killed in the raid. She'd called off their wedding two weeks before the scheduled date.

By the press of his lips and the hollow look in his eyes, Pierce still wasn't over Roxanne or the loss of one of their friends and partners. The botched weapons raid on a warehouse south of town had killed one FBI special agent, two ATF agents and five civilians. It had been an unmitigated disaster, made worse by the fact that both Tuck and Pierce believed some of the criminals behind it were still at large.

"I'll get this video away from here. Bismarck might not be the safest place to unravel the mystery. I'm thinking Skeeter's our man."

"Right. He's got the best equipment and knowledge to do the job. But he's in Minneapolis."

"I'll get it on the soonest flight out and make him understand that it's supersensitive and no one else is to know about it."

Tuck nodded. "Emphasize that we need the data as soon as possible. I'm not sure how long I can keep Julia and Lily hidden."

"You might want to get Julia to look through some mug shots to see if she can identify the killer. That might help us to find him, while we're working on the hard evidence we need to put him away." His brother breathed in and let the breath out slowly. "How will I get in touch with you?"

"I've got a prepaid cell phone. I'll call you."

Pierce plucked a bag of diapers from the shelf. "I believe this is the brand and size on that list."

Tuck's lips quirked upward. "Thanks, brother."

"Don't mention it. And keep my niece safe. I want to meet her soon."

"I'll do my best." Tuck drew in a deep breath, feeling a little less alone in his efforts. Knowing Pierce was out there helping him went a long way toward giving him hope.

Pierce drew his wallet from his pocket and cleaned out every bill, handing it to his brother. "It's not much, but it'll keep you away from the ATMs and credit-card machines." He hugged Tuck again and left.

Tuck gathered the remaining supplies and a baby car seat and headed to the self-checkout, keeping his head down and paying cash for the items.

His pulse thumped against his temple, anxiety making him fumble as he placed the items in a plastic bag and headed for the door. He'd been away for well over an hour. Way too long as far as he was concerned.

What if someone had located Julia and Lily?

All the worst scenarios ran through Tuck's mind as he negotiated the streets, taking a circuitous route back to the obscure bed-and-breakfast motel. He checked and double-checked his rearview mirror at every turn, praying to *Wakantanka* that he wasn't leading the killer back to his wife and baby.

Chapter Eight

Julia's stomach ached from worry, nerves and hunger. The time passed as if in slow motion. Thirty minutes after Tuck left, Lily woke, fussed and finished off the last of the powder formula and the remaining dry diaper. She'd stayed awake for forty minutes, smiling and gurgling, unaware of the trouble she was in. Julia had played with her, tickled her tummy, rocked her and sang softly to keep her from crying.

When Lily fell asleep, Julia glanced at the clock on the nightstand for the hundredth time and flipped on the television, turning the sound off. She wanted to hear what was going on outside, should anyone try to sneak up on her room.

Lily stretched, her face wrinkling, her mouth twisting into a squall. Most likely she had a wet diaper and needed a change.

If Tuck didn't return soon, Julia would be forced to take Lily out of the motel and go in search of needed items. In the meantime, she lifted Lily in her arms and walked into the bathroom in search of a hand towel that might work as a temporary, last-ditch solution to the lack of dry diapers.

With no idea how long Tuck might be gone, Julia decided to make use of her time and take a shower. She and Lily hadn't bathed since before Julia and her sister left for the casino.

A lump lodged in her throat as she recalled how excited she'd been to have a girls' night out with just the two of them. Julia and Jillian had showered, fussed over their hair and driven to the casino for a nice dinner and a night of playing the slots. Jillian hadn't been to visit since her weeklong trip when Lily was born. The FBI had kept her busy on one case after another out of her base in Minneapolis.

Jillian had come to talk Julia into moving with Lily to Minnesota so that she could see them more often.

Julia had considered it on more than one occasion while she'd been pregnant. Yet, she'd stayed in Fort Yates, teaching third grade to the local children. The area was so remote that they were desperate for good teachers.

After graduating from the University of North Dakota in Grand Forks, Julia had taken the job at Fort Yates. The administration had been happy to have her and made her feel welcome in the small community.

Not until she'd met Tuck Thunder Horse on a night out with friends at the casino had she realized just how remote they were and how lonely she'd been for someone else in her life.

But not someone like Tuck.

Not that he wasn't the most handsome man she'd ever met, with his rugged Native American features— high cheekbones, jet-black hair and midnight eyes. But there was more to his attraction than his looks. He had such a powerfully confident way to him—an air of assurance that let everyone who saw him know that he could handle himself in *any* situation.

She'd fallen in love with him after the first dance.

Julia's parents had been introduced by friends and married within a week of their first date—her mother claiming it had been love at first sight. Why not Julia?

Deep down, Julia had always dreamed of meeting the man of her dreams and knowing him on sight. The night she'd met Tuck, it had all been so magical, as if he was the one she was meant to love for the rest of her life.

When he'd asked her to marry him, she'd agreed without hesitation. And if he hadn't been an FBI agent, maybe they could have been happy. But they'd never know that now.

Julia laid Lily across the bathroom counter on a big fluffy towel. Without taking her eyes off the baby for a moment, she fumbled with the shower faucet, turning the fixture to warm. When the temperature was just right for the baby, Julia stripped off her own clothing then the baby's. Holding Lily against her, Julia stepped behind the curtain, letting the water wash down Lily's back.

Her dark-haired, bright-eyed daughter laughed up at her, blinking as water ran down over her head and into her eyes.

Julia held tight as she scrubbed the baby with a soapy washcloth.

When she was finished washing Lily, she perched the naked baby on her hip and worked over her own body with her free hand, squirting shampoo from the miniature bottle provided, slathering her scalp and working suds through the length of her hair. Holding Lily away from her body, she tipped her head back in the water, rinsing her hair free of bubbles.

Lily giggled and squirmed in her arms as she cleaned the remaining soap from both of their bodies.

As she turned off the water, a sound in the other

room made the breath catch in her lungs. Julia pulled the child against her and she remained still on the other side of the shower curtain, afraid to move, to make even the tiniest noise, lest she alert whoever was in the room.

The distinct sound of the motel-room door closing and locking reached her through the hollow bathroom door.

Could it be Tuck? Dared she leave the shower to find out? Or should she stay put and wait until he called out her name?

With Lily clutched against her naked body, water clinging to her skin, chilling her, she waited. No one spoke a word as the sound of muffled movements carried through the room to her, making her nerves jangle and her pulse rocket through her veins.

Say something, Tuck. Let me know it's you, she begged silently.

The handle on the bathroom door jiggled, the metal squeaking as it turned.

Lily wiggled against her and gurgled.

Oh, please, please, please be Tuck, Julia prayed.

A footstep treaded softly on the bathroom tile, barely audible against the noise of blood pounding against Julia's eardrums. She braced herself to leap from the tub and run.

Then the curtain whipped back and a large man towered over her, wearing a black sweatshirt and a black baseball hat pulled down low over his face.

Julia screamed, Lily screamed and the man grabbed them from the tub, pulling them into his arms.

Heart hammering, water dripping from her body, Julia hugged Lily with one arm and fought with the other.

"Damn it, Julia, it's me." The man grunted as her bare foot connected with his shin.

"Tuck?" Julia's gaze shot up to his face, recognizing the high cheekbones and dark skin partially covered by sunglasses and shadowed by the hat's bill. "Oh, thank heavens!"

"What the hell were you doing?" he demanded, his warm hand skimming over her back. "You scared me to death. I thought you'd left."

"I thought you were the murderer." Julia leaned into him, sandwiching Lily between them. "You didn't call out. I didn't know what to do, so I stayed behind the curtain." She buried her face against the dark sweatshirt. "I didn't recognize you behind the glasses…the hat."

He pulled the offending glasses and hat off and tossed them on the counter. "Sorry. I'm just glad you two are all right. I thought you'd been taken."

"No, we just took advantage of the time and got showered." A waft of cold air feathered over her skin, reminding Julia she was naked. She reached for a towel.

Tuck handed it to her, taking Lily from her arms. His gaze never left Julia's body as she reached for the proffered towel. The darkness of his eyes intensified, his body going rigid. Tuck's glance traveled from her ankles all the way to her breasts.

Desire surged through Julia, warming her inside and out. Had he not been holding the baby, she might have forgone the towel…

Her breathing ragged, Julia broke the tension, bringing them back to reality. "Did you bring diapers?"

He shook his head as if clearing her image so that he could focus on something other than her body. "Yes. They're out here."

"Could you dry her and put one on her before she christens you?"

"Would she?" He stared down at the naked baby.

Lily's mouth turned up in a baby grin, and she swatted at his face with a tiny fist.

Tuck smiled back. "You wouldn't do that, would you?" He carried the baby into the other room and laid her on a towel on the bed, talking to her as he tore open the bag of diapers and taped one on her.

Then he peeled off the black sweatshirt, revealing a gray one beneath. He removed that one, too, leaving him in the black T-shirt he'd been wearing when he'd left earlier.

"Is it cold outside?"

"No, the shirts were my disguises to get me in and out of the airport undetected." He turned her way. "It's hot in here."

Julia could practically feel the heat radiating off Tuck's body. She tightened the towel around her, tucking the tail of terry cloth between her breasts.

Tuck's gaze caught the movement, his black eyes smoldering, the tension between them so thick it was palpable.

Convinced he could handle Lily, Julia closed the bathroom door between them and leaned against it, her heart still pounding, her breathing ragged—no longer out of fear, but out of lust for the man in the other room. She had to be crazy to want to make love to him again. Though she wouldn't trade Lily for the world, she didn't relish the consequences of more unprotected sex with the Lakotan. Having faced pregnancy and raising a baby alone, she had no wish to raise another by herself anytime soon.

Julia toweled dry, the textured fabric scraping over

her sensitive nipples, reminding her of how gentle Tuck had been when he'd made love to her a year before. He'd held her, kissed her and brought her to the edge before he'd satisfied his own needs. An attentive lover, he'd known what a woman wanted and wasn't in too much of a hurry to take his time giving it to her.

Her belly tightened, a burning ache swirling at her core. How long would they be on the run, cooped up in tiny quarters, alone together? Julia pressed a hand to her breasts, and her throbbing heart squeezed tightly, taking her back to the day she'd filed the annulment papers.

Back then, she'd put distance between herself and Tuck, firm in her mind about the need to sever all ties. She'd known that the more time she spent with him, the less likely she'd be able to walk away.

Given the current circumstances, she didn't have a choice about staying where she was or going. Tuck was hers and Lily's lifeline. If she wanted to live, she had to stay with him.

Julia dragged in a deep breath and let it out, her skin still tingling, her body on fire from the expression on Tuck's face as he'd devoured her with just one hungry look. Close quarters with the man would prove difficult, if not impossible.

TUCK FOCUSED ON HIS DAUGHTER in an attempt to erase the image of Julia's beautiful naked body. He'd wanted her so badly. He wanted to drag her into his arms again, shove her against the shower wall and drive into her over and over again.

Lily waved a hand in his face, blowing bubbles of drool as if to draw his attention. Her smiles and chubby cheeks quickly distracted him from everything else, and soon he was blowing raspberries on her belly.

The baby girl giggled and clutched at his hair. After playing for a few minutes, she gripped his finger in her tiny fist and dragged it close to her mouth in an attempt to suck on it.

"She's hungry," Tuck called over his shoulder.

"We ran out of formula shortly after you left." Julia stood in the open bathroom door, her body covered from neck to ankle in the oversize sweats Mrs. Glimm had given her. It didn't matter. Even with her hair hanging down in wet ropes, her body swamped in clothing too big for her and her face makeup-free, she was beautiful.

Tuck gritted his teeth as blood rushed south, his jeans becoming painfully tight behind the hard metal zipper. He laid a pillow on each side of where Lily squirmed on the bed to keep her from rolling off. Then he turned his back to Julia and adjusted himself to relieve some of the discomfort before rummaging through the plastic grocery bags to find the can of powdered formula and the water bottles.

Julia took them from him and leveled a scoop of formula into an empty bottle. She filled the baby bottle the rest of the way with water, shook it and handed it to Tuck.

His eyes widened and he held his hands up, refusing to take it. "I need to watch the windows."

"Tell you what—I'll watch out the windows, and you feed your daughter. Unless you're afraid of a baby?"

He frowned. "I'm not afraid of my daughter." However, he wasn't sure he was ready to do more than change a diaper. He gathered Lily into his arms, sat on the side of the bed and held out his hand for the bottle. "What do I do?"

"Stick it in her mouth. She knows what to do next. All you have to do is hold her."

"What if she chokes?"

"She won't." Julia smiled. "You'll do fine."

One hand on the bottle, the other holding Lily against his chest, Tuck tapped the nipple against the baby's lips.

Lily opened her mouth and greedily sucked in the rubber tip, pulling hard to start the flow of milk. For fifteen minutes, he cradled his daughter, a surge of love like he'd never known filling every corner of his soul. In the brief time he'd known of his daughter, he finally understood how his mother could have given up a life in the city to spend it raising four rowdy boys.

Lily finished the last drop of the formula and drifted off to sleep, her long black eyelashes resting against her smooth baby cheeks.

Tuck's heart swelled, his chest so tight he could barely breathe. "She's beautiful." He'd never experienced anything as painfully wonderful as holding his own child in his arms. "Thank you for having her."

"I was pregnant. What other choice was there?"

"You could have aborted her."

Julia shook her head. "No."

Tuck stood and laid the baby on the bed between two pillows, a fist tightening around his heart as he stared down at the tiny being who'd quickly become an essential part of his life, his heart and his family. "Given the circumstances, some women would have considered it."

"Not me," Julia whispered. She hadn't moved since she'd come to stand in the doorway of the bathroom.

Tuck was surprised to see tears in her eyes and a trail of them trickling across her cheeks. He took the step that closed the distance between them and brushed a thumb across her skin.

Julia looked up at him through glistening blue eyes. "I'm sorry, Tuck. I should have told you about Lily.

You had a right to know your daughter." She inhaled and let the breath out slowly. "And she had a right to know her father."

"At least I can hold her now."

Julia nodded. "When this…is all over, I'll make sure you get to see her often. We'll work out a schedule for weekends, holidays…"

The Thunder Horses were a tight-knit clan. They protected their loved ones with their lives. How could he take care of his daughter and his daughter's mother when they'd be so far away most of the time? "What if weekends and holidays are not enough?"

Julia frowned. "I can't give her up. She's my life, a part of me."

Frustration simmered low in his belly, surging upward. "Lily is my daughter. She's a Thunder Horse. She looks like us—you said so yourself."

"But she's my baby," Julia cried, her eyes wide, her voice catching on a sob. "I could never leave her."

He stepped in closer, looming over her. "She's mine, too. I want her in my life. I want her to live where I can watch over her, protect her."

Julia stiffened, her mouth forming a thin line, her eyes narrowing. She backed up a few steps so she wouldn't have to tip her head to look him in the eye. "I want to protect her, too. I'd give my life for her, and I'm more prepared to back it up."

Tuck stared across at Julia. "What do you mean by that?"

"I'll always be there for her." She squared her shoulders, her chin held high. "Can you say the same?"

"Yes, damn it." He shook his head. "Why wouldn't I?"

"As a teacher, I won't constantly be in danger. I don't

go to work each day with the possibility of not coming home to my family. Can you guarantee you won't be killed in the line of duty?"

Tuck opened his mouth, *Hell yeah* poised on his tongue. But he couldn't say it when it wasn't altogether true.

Julia nodded, another tear slipping from the corner of her eye. "Will you protect your daughter from the heartache of losing her father to a criminal's bullet?" Julia's voice shook. "What happens when I have to tell Lily her daddy won't be around to go to her games, to teach her to ride a bicycle or horse, to walk her down the aisle at her wedding? Who will be there to hold her when her heart breaks?"

Lily whimpered and stirred on the mattress.

His own heart breaking at each word Julia uttered, Tuck closed the distance and pulled her against him, pressing his face into the curve of her neck. "No. I can't guarantee I'll always be there."

Her hands rose and fell to her sides. "Exactly."

When she tried to back away, Tuck refused to let go. "I can't guarantee I'll always be there, but I can guarantee I'll always love her and provide for her whether I'm there or not."

Julia stared into his face and used his own words. "What if that's not enough? What if she wants more?"

For a long moment Tuck stared into Julia's face, then he let go. "Is that why you left?" he asked softly, a hint of understanding lacing his words.

Julia nodded, her bottom lip trembling. "My father was an FBI agent. We lost him when I was twelve. He wasn't there with me when I graduated high school. He wasn't there when Jillian graduated from Quantico. I watched my mother die a slow death because of a broken heart. And now I've lost the only family I had left besides Lily." She shook her head. "When I found your badge…I knew I couldn't stay married to you. I can't do it. I can't give my heart to someone who might die tomorrow."

Tuck struggled to find words to convince her that those things wouldn't happen to him, but they wouldn't be completely true. He loved his work with the FBI. He had always wanted to be part of the bureau and knew the risks associated. Having just lost a close friend in a botched raid, he had an even better understanding of his own mortality.

His gaze shifted from Lily back to Julia. He couldn't give up his career for them—but how could he let them go? Was there anything he could say to change Julia's mind? "No one can guarantee he'll be here tomorrow. Who's to say any one of us won't die in a car wreck?" He took a step toward her.

Julia backed away again, running up against the wall. "The chances are higher of a special agent dying in the line of duty than dying from a vehicle accident."

"What if I was a pilot? A soldier? A construction worker?" He cupped her face with his palms and forced her to look him in the eyes. "Would you have left me?"

She shook her head. "I don't know. We were foolish, marrying after knowing each other only a night."

"Weren't you the one who said you believed in love at first sight?" He tucked her hair back behind her ear. "You felt something, otherwise you wouldn't have said yes."

"Lust," she said, her gaze dropping to his lips. "It was lust."

Tuck nodded. "I'll grant you I felt that, too, but it was more than lust." His lips hovered over hers. "More than

craving the feeling of your naked body against mine."
He brushed a featherlight kiss across her lips, savoring
the softness, the taste, the warmth of her breath. "Can
you deny it?"

Her breath hitched, her hands rising to his waist,
fingers sliding beneath the T-shirt. "No. But it changes
nothing."

"It sure as hell does." His mouth crashed down on
hers, his arms crushing her against him. Maybe he
wanted to prove a point with the kiss, but the point
backfired, making him want her more than ever.

His fingers slid beneath her sweatshirt, skimming
across her ribs and up to her lacy bra. He flicked the
catch behind her back, releasing her breasts into his
palms.

Julia's nails dug into his skin, her back arching,
pressing her body into his.

Grabbing the hem of her shirt, he ripped it up over
her head and tossed it to the dresser.

She lowered her arms, her bra straps sliding down.
With a flick of her wrist, she flung the bra to land on
the dresser, then grabbed Tuck's shirt, pushing it up
over his head.

Her fingers smoothed across his naked chest, her
gaze following her movements as her hands lifted to his
face. She cupped his cheek, her thumb brushing across
his lip. Then she rose on her tiptoes and kissed him.

Tuck returned the pressure, running his hands down
her back to the top of the elastic waistband of the oversize sweatpants, sending a silent thank-you to Mrs.
Glimm for the easy-on, easy-off garment. With a quick
jerk, he had the pants and her panties down around her
ankles.

Julia stepped free, her leg circling behind his, sliding up his thigh.

Tuck reached behind her and lifted her, wrapping her legs around his waist. He braced her back against the wall and sucked the tip of one of her full, ripe breasts into his mouth.

Her head tipped back, her long, damp hair sliding down over her shoulders. She moaned, pressing her fingers to his nape, urging him to take more.

He obliged, sucking the tip in, pulling hard, his tongue flicking over the taut nipple.

Julia moaned, her legs tightening around his middle, the apex of her thighs rubbing over the ridge of the jeans that had become unbearably tight.

Tuck reached beneath her naked bottom, released the button of his jeans and ripped down the zipper, freeing his member.

Pushing up with her arms, Julia came down over him, pausing with his tip pressing against her entrance.

"No." Tuck set her away, sliding her bottom onto the dresser's surface. He stood between her legs, his fingers tracing a line from the backs of her knees up the inside of her thighs. "Not yet."

"Don't take too long. I want you," she whispered. "Inside me."

He leaned into her, pressing a kiss to her lips. "Patience."

His mouth moved over her lips, his tongue delving between her teeth to swirl around hers. Breaking the kiss, he tongued and nipped a path from her lips to her earlobe and down the long, sleek line of her neck, pushing aside tendrils of hair to reach the skin beneath.

Her chest rose and fell erratically with each touch, her breasts rubbing against him. He pinched a nipple between his thumb and forefinger, rolling the tip, while sucking the other into his mouth.

Julia moaned, her bottom squirming against the laminated wood. Her fingers laced through his hair, dragging him closer.

He left her breasts, moving down over her ribs and lower still to the thatch of curly hair covering her sex.

Her hands skimmed across his back, nails biting into his skin, her moans thick with desire.

Dropping to his knees, Tuck slipped his fingers into her curls. He parted her folds and tongued the swollen nubbin at the center.

Julia bucked, her back arching, her hands clutching the back of his head.

When he flicked his tongue over her again, she cried out, "Please, don't."

"Does this hurt?" Tuck barely touched her this time and she came unglued.

"Yes… No! Oh, heavens, it feels so good."

"Then why stop?"

"It's too good. I think I might come apart."

Ignoring her protest, he laved her, stroking her center again and again, eliciting more cries, more moans until her body stiffened and she tugged at his hair.

He glanced up at her face.

Julia's eyes were squeezed tightly shut, her cheeks a rosy red, her mouth curved in a tight O.

His own senses on fire, Tuck stood and pressed his shaft to her opening.

Her eyes opened wide, her breath hitching. "Please tell me you have protection."

Holding her against him, he reached into the bag on the dresser and removed a box of condoms.

Julia's brows dipped, her blue eyes still glazed.

With a half smile, Tuck handed her the box. "I wasn't planning on seducing you, if that's what you think. I just knew how I felt about being with a woman as tempting as you are, and I didn't want to be caught unprepared this time."

She didn't say a word, instead ripping the box open, dumping its contents into her hand. She selected a foil packet and tore it open with her teeth and unrolled the rubber down over his length.

Then she wrapped her legs around his back, crossing her ankles, bringing him close enough to thrust in, but hesitating at the last minute.

Tuck's breath caught and held in his throat, his blood burning through his veins, his member throbbing, eager and ready to take her.

"Just so you know…" She sucked in a deep breath, her ankles tightening ever so slightly, allowing his tip to slide into her juices. "This changes nothing." Her thighs clenched, her calves pulling him close.

Tuck thrust into her warm, wet channel, filling her, sliding deep.

Tuck closed his eyes, relishing the sensations rocketing through his system, threatening to make him explode at the slightest movement. He held back, refusing to come too soon, wanting to please her, to bring her back to the brink before he shattered into a million pieces.

He pulled back and plunged in again, setting a fast, steady rhythm that matched the thundering beat of his heart.

As the tension built in Tuck, Julia's hands curled around his hips, driving him faster, deeper, harder until he pitched over the edge. He thrust one last time, holding her as close as was humanly possible, his member throbbing inside her.

When he came back to earth, the full force of what he'd done hit him. He'd taken this woman for the second time.

He'd been fooling himself thinking he could resist, believing that a passion as powerful and consuming as theirs could be ignored or forgotten. This encounter only proved what he'd known the night he asked her to marry him. Julia belonged with him.

She'd said it changed nothing, but she was so very wrong.

Now all he had to do was convince her.

Chapter Nine

Julia remained in Tuck's arms, staying connected to him in the most intimate way for as long as she possibly could. Breaking apart would mean the end of something so beautiful she'd almost forgotten everything else.

Tuck was the first to return to reality. He was nuzzling her neck when his head came up with a jerk, his eyes wide open, his ears cocked toward the door.

"What's wrong? Did you hear something?" Julia asked, reluctant to bring an end to their lovemaking, even as fear shot adrenaline into her bloodstream and raised gooseflesh on her skin.

Tuck sucked in a deep breath and pulled free, his member glistening in the dim lighting. He rapidly disposed of the condom, then dragged his jeans up over his hips and zipped them, moving toward the window at the same time.

Carefully nudging aside the corner of the curtain, he peered out.

Julia grabbed the towel from the bathroom floor, wrapped it around herself and joined Tuck at the window.

A dark car with heavily tinted windows pulled into the narrow parking lot, stopped, waited for several seconds, then backed up and drove away.

Tuck yanked his T-shirt over his head, pulled the gray sweatshirt on after and covered his hair with a hat. "Stay here. I'll be right back. Don't open the door for anyone but me."

Julia's pulse sped, her hand shaking as she tugged the curtain back in place.

Tuck edged the door open a crack, looked out then slipped through, closing it quietly behind him.

Her breath catching in her throat, Julia locked the dead bolt and slipped the chain in place, then she pulled aside the curtain again.

Within seconds, Tuck disappeared around the corner of the building.

Julia's hand froze on the fabric, her body trembling, dread pushing all thoughts from her head but fear for Tuck's safety.

Fortunately, a tiny sigh from the baby sleeping on the bed behind her was all it took to force Julia out of her panic attack and into action. If Tuck ran into a real threat, Julia needed to be prepared to run or defend. Whichever it was, she couldn't do it in a towel.

She snatched the panties and sweatpants from the floor and jerked them up her thighs. Clipping her bra around her middle, she guided the straps over her shoulders, then dragged on the sweatshirt.

Julia shoved her feet into her shoes and threw the supplies Tuck had brought into the backpack, her nerves jumping at every sound she heard or imagined. She finger-combed her hair into some sense of order, braided the damp strands and wound the braid around the crown of her head, tucking it beneath the baseball cap.

Lily slept soundly, her pretty little mouth moving in a sucking motion. With a full tummy, dry diaper and warm blanket, she was completely comfortable and at peace, blissfully unaware of the danger her mommy and daddy faced. She didn't need much to make her happy.

She didn't know the heartache of losing a loved one. Lily wouldn't know what it was like to fall in love for many years to come, and when she did, Julia hoped she didn't fall for an FBI special agent.

As hard as Julia had tried to forget Tuck during the long nine months of pregnancy, once Lily was born, her daughter served as a daily reminder of the man. She looked so much like him it had hurt Julia more than she'd ever imagined to gaze down into her daughter's face.

She couldn't count how often she'd second-guessed her frenzied rush to sever all ties with Tuck Thunder Horse. Now, seeing Lily with Tuck, the way he held her as if she was precious china, smoothing a finger over her cheek, blowing raspberries at her belly, gave Julia pause. He'd cooed and talked to her daughter with that deep, warm tone that sent shivers all over Julia's body.

In the short time they'd been together since her sister's death, Julia felt the walls she'd built beginning to crumble, and it scared her so much her knees trembled.

After the mind-blowing sex they'd just indulged in, Julia knew it would be much harder walking away from Tuck Thunder Horse this time.

When she had everything ready to go, she paced the floor, finally perching on the edge of the bed, her hand resting on her daughter, ready to snatch her up and run if necessary. The clock on the nightstand ticked another minute. One more since the last time she'd glanced at it. What was taking him so long?

A soft knock brushed against the door.

Julia leaped to her feet and dashed to answer, her hand reaching for the handle before she stopped, fingers poised over the knob. At the last moment, she pressed her eye to the peephole.

Tuck's dark countenance stared back at her. "It's me. Open up."

Julia yanked the chain loose and twisted the dead bolt, flinging open the door.

Tuck stepped in and closed the door.

Before she could think, Julia threw her arms around Tuck. "Thank God you're back."

He chuckled and held her close, then he skimmed his lips across hers and set her away, glancing around the room with a quick, appraising look. "Good, you're packed."

"We're leaving?" Julia reached for Lily, gathering her daughter into her arms.

"I don't trust the driver of the car that just passed through. The clerk at the front desk said a man had been asking her if a blonde had checked in with a baby."

The air left Julia's lungs. "They've found us?"

"Not necessarily. Remember, you weren't with me when I registered. As far as the clerk knows, only a single man is renting this room. I didn't tell her any different."

"Then we're safe."

"No. That was too close for comfort. Whoever is after you is canvassing the hotels in Bismarck. It won't be long before someone sees you and Lily and word gets back."

"Where can we hide and not be seen?"

"I know of a place, but we'll be roughing it."

"As long as Lily's safe, warm and dry, I don't care." She headed for the door.

Tuck blocked her. "You wait inside with Lily and let

BUSINESS REPLY MAIL
FIRST-CLASS MAIL   PERMIT NO. 717   BUFFALO, NY

POSTAGE WILL BE PAID BY ADDRESSEE

THE READER SERVICE
PO BOX 1867
BUFFALO NY 14240-9952

NO POSTAGE
NECESSARY
IF MAILED
IN THE
UNITED STATES

me go first." He carried the backpack out to the rental car parked around the back of the motel.

When he returned, he took Lily and led the way to the car. In the backseat, he'd installed an infant car seat, locked down by the middle safety belt. He'd added shades on each of the back side windows. He buckled Lily in and drew a baby blanket up to her chin.

Taking her position in the passenger seat, Julia pulled her cap low over her eyes, glancing over the seat at Tuck working the straps.

Once the baby was settled, Tuck slid into the driver's seat and backed out.

Julia held her breath as they ventured out of the motel parking lot onto the street, feeling like a fugitive on the lam from the law. Once the crime lab identified her sister as Jillian Anderson, not Julia, she could probably count on the Sioux County sheriff bumping her to the top of the suspects list, possibly putting out an all-points bulletin to bring her in for questioning. Then she *would* be a fugitive both from the law and from the killer. She had no intention of turning herself over to the authorities until they figured out who had killed her sister.

Jillian, oh, Jillian. How could you leave me in such a mess?

As Tuck pulled away from the motel, Julia sat quietly in the seat beside him, missing her sister so badly her heart ached and moisture blurred her vision.

For fifteen minutes, she remained silent, willing the tears to go away. She had to be strong, to keep it together for Lily. When she finally looked up, the city had faded away to farmland as they sped across the countryside.

"Where are we going?"

"Somewhere safe. A place they won't find us."

She snorted. "Where would that be?"

"The Thunder Horse Ranch."

"Your home?" Julia's heart skipped several beats and settled into an erratic rhythm. "Isn't that a couple hours away?"

"It'll take a little more than three hours to get there. But I can't think of anyplace I can keep you safer. I know the land, the places to hide and how to survive. We'll stay in a hunting cabin out on the range. No one will know we're there but my brother Pierce. The killer won't know how to find us. You and Lily will be safe."

Tuck pulled the prepaid cell phone from his pocket and keyed in a number. "Pierce, we're on our way to the ranch." He paused. "We'll stick to the back roads. Don't worry. I'll call as soon as I can." He hit the end button and tucked the phone back into his pocket. "Pierce agreed that it's a good idea to get you two out of Bismarck."

"How will we continue the investigation from the back of beyond?" She faced Tuck, reaching out to lay her hand on his sleeve. "We can't abandon the search for Jillian's killer. Lily and I won't be safe until he's captured."

"Pierce will continue the investigation with the help of our guy in Minneapolis. We can't risk Lily's life to find your sister's murderer. We have to trust the FBI agents we're working with to do their jobs."

Julia leaned back in her seat, her heart sick at Tuck's arbitrary decision. "I feel like we're letting down Jillian." She stared straight ahead at the endless flat terrain interspersed with farm fields and prairie.

She wanted to scream and rant and yell at him for dragging her even farther away from those who'd taken her sister's life. But a glance in the backseat reaffirmed her number-one priority.

Lily.

The baby slept in the car seat, her head tipped to one side, a smile twitching at the corners of her mouth.

Julia would do anything to keep her daughter safe.

"How long will we be there?" she asked, her voice flat, emotionless. The farther away from Fort Yates they went, the more she felt as if she'd failed her sister.

"As long as it takes to extract and analyze that video."

"What if they don't recover the video off the phone?" she asked. "What if that leaves me as the only witness to the crime and the only one who saw what was on the video?" Her voice faded. She clenched her hands in her lap to keep them from shaking.

"We'll cross that bridge if it happens. For now we have to have faith that the techies will be able to recover enough to find the person responsible."

In other words, he didn't have an answer.

Julia had been afraid of that. If she was the only witness to the NIGC agent's murder, the killer would want to make sure he tied up all of the loose ends. She'd never be safe and neither would Lily.

She had one of two choices. She could wallow in self-pity or be strong and see to her daughter's well-being. Julia sat up straight and stared ahead, making a mental list of what they'd require to survive in a remote cabin for any length of time. "We'll need enough supplies to last a few days."

"The cabin has a stock of canned foods."

"We'll need more formula and bottled water for Lily. And diapers. That little bag you got won't go far."

"We can stop in one of the small towns before we get to the ranch and load up."

"Good. I could use a pair of jeans and a jacket." She sat forward and watched for a general store that would have the things they needed to rough it for as long as necessary.

Avoiding the interstate highway, they followed the old farm roads. An hour and a half out of Bismarck, they eased into the little community of Hazen.

Julia pointed ahead. "Drop me at that general store. I'll shop for what I need. You can gas up."

As she climbed out of the car, she opened the back door to collect Lily.

"Leave her in the car seat. She can sleep while I put fuel in the car."

Julia hesitated. Given the circumstances, she didn't want to let Lily out of her sight. But her daughter was with her daddy. He'd protect her. "Okay. I'll only be a few minutes."

"When I'm done, I'll join you. I'm sure there are things I need to get, as well."

Hurrying into the store, Julia looked back at the sedan as Tuck pulled away. The shades over the back windows made it impossible for her to see Lily.

A hollowness settled around her heart as Julia forced herself to turn away. Tuck would take care of Lily while Julia did the necessary shopping.

With her luck, the cabin probably didn't have plumbing or electricity, so besides formula, water and diapers, Julia loaded her cart with candles, flashlights, toilet paper, matches and canned goods, praying they at least had a can opener. She selected a pair of jeans and a sweatshirt for herself to augment the oversize sweat suit Mrs. Glimm had given her. Her own clothing was still damp from the morning's attempt to hand-wash them. If she didn't get them hung to dry soon, they'd mildew and be ruined.

Ten minutes later Julia waited by the register, peering out the window in search of Tuck. She didn't have enough money to pay for the items and had hoped he'd arrive in time to cover the charges. Where was he?

Another five minutes passed and Julia had gone from mildly annoyed to worried.

Her first conclusion to jump to was that he'd driven off with Lily, leaving her to fend for herself in Hazen.

No, he wouldn't have done that. Not after having risked his life to save her and to bring her as far as he had.

The next conclusion Julia leaped to was that he was in trouble. And if Tuck was in jeopardy, Lily would be, too.

Abandoning her cart, Julia pushed through the door and ran down the road to the gas station. They'd seen the sign for it from the road, and Tuck had indicated that was where he'd go when he'd said he'd be filling up.

The rental car wasn't in front of a pump, and a closed sign hung in the window, the insides bare and deserted. Tuck, the sedan and Lily were nowhere to be seen.

Julia fought to breathe, her heart hammering, her lungs constricting. *Calm down,* she willed herself. He'd just gone on to another station, this one being closed. She spun in a three-hundred-and-sixty-degree circle, the buildings, gas pumps and cars moving by in a dizzying haze.

Where were they?

She started down the street in a stumbling daze, tears welling in her eyes, blinding her. No matter how many times she told herself to get a grip, she couldn't. Dread settled like a wad of bile burning a hole in the pit of her gut.

Through her watery view, Julia spotted a dark gray sedan parked beside a large, rusted trash container, at the rear of a gas station farther down the street. Hope leaped into her throat and she sprinted the remaining block, ignoring the strange glances from people she passed.

It has to be them, she chanted, her heart refusing to beat, her breathing caught firmly in her lungs. When she came close to the car, she recognized the license plate. It was the car Mr. Glimm had rented for them. The driver's door hung open, and a gray-sweatshirt-clad arm dangled out, the hand limp and lifeless.

Julia swayed, her footsteps foundering to an unsteady halt. She had to force herself forward, afraid of what she'd find. The nightmare of her sister's death reared up to taunt her.

A groan sounded from inside the car and the hand clenched.

Hope surged, shoving Julia forward.

Tuck was slumped against the steering wheel. An egg-size knot swelled on the back of his head, blood congealing on the collar of the gray sweatshirt. But he groaned again, the sound like angels singing to Julia's desperate soul. Tuck was alive.

Her thoughts immediately swung to her baby. She yanked open the back door and the bottom dropped out of her world.

The backseat was empty. Car seat, backpack and baby…gone.

Julia dropped to her knees, her face turning upward to the sky. "Dear God, please. Not my baby."

Chapter Ten

Stabbing pain radiated from the back of Tuck's skull all the way through to his teeth. A moaning wail roused him from the fog of unconsciousness to semiconscious. The sound was so forlorn it made his heart ache for the person crying.

He sat up straight and fought a heavy wave of nausea and dizziness, unconsciousness threatening to claim him again. He had to stay awake. Someone needed him. For several long moments, he struggled to remember who that someone was.

Then it all came back to him. The gas station, the men wearing ski masks and carrying guns, the threat and Lily.

Tuck's eyes jerked open and he spun in his seat to peer into the back, a ton of lead landing hard in the hollow of his belly. Lily was gone.

Another moan rose from the pavement beside the car.

Tuck swung a leg out of the car, then another. When both feet rested on the ground, he pushed upward, his arms bracing on the car for balance and support.

As he straightened, the throbbing at the base of his skull intensified, but the fog of dizziness decreased. He rounded the open back door and felt the sucker punch of failure hit him full in the chest.

Julia lay crumpled on the ground, her shoulders shuddering with deep, heart-wrenching sobs.

His head hurting so badly it brought tears to his eyes, Tuck dropped to his knees beside her and gathered her in his arms. "Oh, God, Julia. I'm sorry."

"She's gone." Julia sobbed into his sweatshirt, her tears soaking through to his skin.

"We'll get her back. I swear to you we'll get her back." He held her close, the ache in his chest far more excruciating than the one on the back of his head.

When the sobs subsided, Julia clutched the front of his shirt and stared up at him, her eyes swollen and desperate. "What did the kidnappers say? Did they leave a note? Instructions? Anything?"

He tentatively rubbed the back of his head, trying to remember exactly what they'd told him before knocking him on the back of the head with a tire iron. When the full extent of their demands filled his memory, his fists clenched into tight knots. "They want the recording and you in exchange for Lily."

"Did you tell them we didn't have it?" Julia clung to him.

"I told them it was at least five hours away." Tuck pressed his fingers to his temple. "We have to get it back from Minneapolis, fast."

"My God, they have Lily." Julia squeezed her eyes closed. "Assuming we can get the phone back that soon, how am I supposed to get the video to them? How will we contact them? Who will be taking care of my baby?"

Tuck's head ached, his eyes blurring from the pain. "They said to have the cell phone by midnight in Bismarck and they'll contact us with instructions. We're not to talk to anyone, police or FBI."

"We have to give them whatever it takes. Lily isn't

leverage to be traded like money or gold." Julia's voice caught on a sob. "She's a baby—she won't understand. They won't be patient when she cries. We have to get her back. Now."

Guilt tore at Tuck, making him hurt as if he'd been beaten all over with that tire iron. "We can't do anything until they contact us again."

"Why? Can't we go after them? Stop them?"

"They hold all the cards. They have Lily. They warned me that if we followed, they'd hurt Lily."

"Oh, God." Julia pressed her knuckles to her lips, more tears falling. "She's just a baby."

"They have to make the next move and contact us."

"But how?" She scrubbed an arm across her face.

"They'll call me on my cell phone."

She pushed to her feet, her eyes wide, her grip on his hand tight. "We have to call the cops. I should have done that in the first place."

"We can't, Julia. Not unless we're willing to risk Lily getting…" Tuck couldn't finish the sentence. The thought of anything bad happening to Lily made his stomach roil and his anger skyrocket. If they hurt his daughter, he'd kill the bastards, ripping them apart, one limb at a time. The more pain he could inflict, the better.

"Oh, Tuck. I should have given that recording to the police as soon as Jillian sent it to me." She leaned her forehead against his chest. "It's my fault. None of this would have happened if I hadn't insisted Jillian and I go to the casino that night. Jillian would be alive, Lily would be home in her bed and I'd be teaching third graders. I'm cursed."

Tuck grabbed her arms and shook her gently. "You are not cursed. You're a beautiful woman with a lot to live for. Number one, your daughter will need her mother when we get her back."

"She'll have her father."

"And what good have I been to her? They found us and took her right out of my protection. Some bodyguard I am."

Julia stared into his eyes, her own tears ceasing to flow. "Okay, you've made your point. We're both at fault, and crying about it isn't getting Lily back. We have to *do* something."

"Right. Come on. I need to make a phone call, then we need to get back to Bismarck as quickly as possible."

"We can't get to Minneapolis and back in five hours."

"No, but Pierce can have the phone sent on the first plane out."

"In the meantime, what will we do?"

"We're going to do the best we can to catch a killer and get Lily back." He led her around the car to the passenger side.

"What do you mean?" Julia dug her heels into the pavement, a frown settling between her brows. "We have to do exactly as they say. We're going to get that phone and trade it and me to get Lily back. I won't play Russian roulette with my daughter's life."

"No. I won't let you trade yourself for Lily. We have five hours between now and the time we have to make the exchange. As far as I'm concerned, we need to make full use of that five hours to find out who is behind this and why. Hopefully, our guy in Minneapolis has downloaded the data and is looking at it now. We'll figure this out. I know we will."

"Tuck, we can't let them analyze it. If they do and the killer finds out, he'll kill Lily."

"We bought time to get the phone back. In the meantime, we need to get *you* to our field office to see if you can identify the murderer by looking through our criminal database. If you can identify him, we might not need the video. We might be able to find him before the exchange takes place."

Julia chewed on her lip, but finally nodded. "Okay. If you really think it will get us to Lily faster, I'll do it."

"Good girl." Tuck pulled out the cell phone he'd purchased back in Bismarck and dialed his brother. "Pierce, they took Lily."

"What happened?"

"We stopped in a little town an hour and a half northwest of Bismarck for fuel and groceries for the next couple days. They jumped me while I was getting gas." He didn't add how they'd held a gun pointed at Lily. Tuck had had no choice but to let them take her.

"Did you get a good look at them?" Pierce asked.

"No. They wore ski masks and carried SIG Sauers."

"Where's Julia?"

He glanced across at the mother of his child. Her face had paled with the retelling of the details. "Julia's with me. They want her and the cell phone in exchange for the baby." Tuck held out his hand and took hers.

Her fingers were cold, her hands trembling in his. He was proud of her for holding it together as well as she was, considering her child was missing and in danger.

"Pierce, I need the phone back in Bismarck ASAP. I have to be ready when they call me about the transfer."

"I'll see what I can do. I don't know if Skeeter's had time to pull the data off it or if he's had a chance to analyze it."

"At this point, it might be best if he hasn't done either. They didn't want Julia to share the data with anyone. We can't risk the baby's life. See if you can call in a favor or two and get a plane. I don't know how desperate these people are." Tuck's hand tightened around Julia's. "Call me when you get Julia's phone to Bismarck."

"I'm on it," Pierce said. "Be safe, brother."

"I will. You, too." Tuck clicked the phone off and pulled Julia into his arms. "We *will* get her back."

THE DRIVE BACK TO BISMARCK sped by in a haze, the road blurring in front of the vehicle as Tuck broke every speed limit between Hazen and North Dakota's capital city.

Julia clutched the armrests, for once unafraid of the speed, more frightened of what might be happening with Lily.

Tuck drove through the residential streets, steering clear of major thoroughfares. He seemed to drive in circles until he finally pulled onto a dirt road leading to what appeared to be the back portion of a public park.

He hid the car in the shadows of a stand of young aspens.

A man jogged by on a dirt path thirty feet away.

"I come here to jog on nice days when the ground is dry." Tuck stared out the window, his gaze following the progress of the lone runner.

"How long will we have to stay here?"

"Until after everyone leaves the office."

She checked the clock on the dash, her foot tapping the floor. The longer Lily was away from her, the more anxious she got. It was already past her feeding time, and she probably needed a diaper change. Would her captors take care of her? Would she be all right? "When will everyone be out?"

"I'm going to find out right now." Tuck pulled out

the prepaid phone and dialed. "Give me Josh Behling's desk."

"Tuck here." He listened for a moment. "Yeah, I know I owe him an explanation, but the boss can wait. Tell him I'm working on the case and have a lead... anything. Just keep him off my back for a little while longer. I've got too much riding on me now." Another pause. "I figured they would by now. Yup, Julia and Jillian were identical twins." He shook his head, staring out at the jogging track. "They did? Damn." Tuck's jaw tightened, a little tic twitching in his cheek.

Julia listened to the one-sided conversation, holding her breath to better hear what was being said on the other end. It didn't help; she couldn't make out the words. She wanted to know what Behling had said to cause Tuck's reaction.

"Look, Behling, we have to get inside the office to the computers." He listened, his brows furrowing. "I know it's risky, but I need to bring Julia in to let her look through our database and see if she can identify the killer." He nodded. "Yeah. I hate to ask it, but I can't see any other way, and time is critical. They kidnapped the baby, and they're holding her hostage, demanding Julia in exchange."

Julia's heart flipped over at the mention of Lily. All the worry welled up in her, pushing against her chest cavity, making her hurt so bad she thought she was having a heart attack.

"No. If Julia surrenders to the police, we may not get Lily back alive. Okay, just let me know when the coast is clear. Thanks."

When he pressed the end button, he stared out at the encroaching night.

Julia gave him several seconds of silence, her curiosity killing her. Finally, she blurted, "What did Josh say that made you swear?"

"They identified the body as Jillian's." He spoke quietly, his tone soft and respectful of the pain it might cause her.

"You figured they would, right?" Julia gulped back the ready tears. "What else?"

"They have an APB out for you. They want to bring you in for questioning." He glanced across at her. "I'm sorry."

"It's not your fault. They were likely to jump to that conclusion anyway. I read somewhere the statistics show that a high number of murders are performed by family members or someone the victim knows. Not that that explains the death of the NIGC representative, but they have to figure I at least saw something—and might have been involved. With me skipping town, they were bound to mark me as a person of interest."

Tuck reached out and skimmed a finger along Julia's jaw. "You're amazing, you know that? I don't see how you hold it together."

She leaned into his hand, the warmth on her cool cheek giving her hope. "I have to keep it together... for Lily."

His hand dropped to his side and he turned away. "The FBI regional director flew in when he heard it was one of his agents from Minneapolis. He's mad about what happened to Jillian and wants a head on a platter yesterday."

Julia gulped. "Mine?"

Tuck shook his head. "He wants answers."

With a gentle snort, Julia commented, "Don't we all?" She hugged her arms around her middle and glanced into the distance, counting the minutes until

Josh called to give them the all clear. "What if I can't identify the killer from the million photos you must have in your database?" She shivered, scraping her memory for an image, the one she'd glimpsed as a man put a bullet through another. Had she seen his face clearly enough to recognize him? It all happened so fast. The video had been helpful in reminding her about his appearance, giving her a profile and hair color. She remembered that he'd had a streak of white on one side. But she'd watched the video only once. And with all the stress and anxiety of the past day, she wasn't sure how clear her memory would be. Would it be enough to pick him out of hundreds of images?

"Then we'll wait until we hear back from Lily's captors. Maybe the call will give us something to go on." Tuck's voice sounded strained. The fingers holding the steering wheel were gripping so tightly, his knuckles were turning white.

Julia wanted to soothe his nerves, but hers were already strung so tight she might snap at any moment. "I hate being at their mercy. I feel completely helpless."

"Me, too. But we don't have to wait around for Pierce's contact to recover the video or for Pierce to get the cell phone back to us. We can be more proactive by finding the killer sooner, if possible."

Butterflies flipped in her belly. "I don't know if I'll recognize him."

"You have to try."

"How do you propose to get me into the office building?" Julia asked. "Doesn't the FBI building have restricted access?"

"Leave that to me. I'll get you past the guard at the desk."

Julia glanced across at Tuck. He had it together, his

face lined with worry but set in fierce determination. If anyone could get Lily back, it would be Tuck. Darkness filtered in around them, the night melding shadows together.

The phone in the console buzzed.

Julia jumped, her pulse leaping into high gear.

Tuck snatched up the phone and hit the talk button. "Okay, we'll be there in a few minutes. Call if the situation changes."

He tossed the phone into the cup holder and turned the key in the ignition. "Ready?"

"I want my baby back." Julia buckled her seat belt and held on. "Let's do it."

Tuck backed out of the cover of the bushes and merged into traffic on the interstate, taking the Washington Street exit, headed north. He turned right on Broadway, the streets of Bismarck as familiar as his hometown of Medora. The huge concrete building housing the Bismarck satellite office of the FBI stood between Fourth and Fifth streets. He parked in front.

Julia's heartbeat stuttered, then settled into an erratic, panicked beat. "Aren't we conspicuous out here?"

Tuck opened her door and helped her out. "You're my person of interest. I'm bringing you in for questioning."

Julia gasped and stared up into his eyes. Had he betrayed her?

His mouth tightened. "Go with me on this, and maybe we'll walk in and out, no problems."

With a nod, she allowed him to hook her elbow and steer her through the glass entry. Tuck flashed his credentials and they walked past the guard, climbed into the elevator and sped up to the floor where he had an office.

A man waited for them, his gaze darting around them and to the four corners of the room.

Tuck shook hands with the man. "Thanks, Behling. I owe you."

"Come with me. I have a computer booted, the system up and waiting." Behling spun without waiting for a response.

Tuck followed, his hand firmly on Julia's arm.

A cold blast of fear washed over her as they zigzagged down corridors and past office cubicles until they reached one marked Tuck Thunder Horse. As Tuck rounded the corner, another figure stepped out of the shadows.

Julia stifled a scream, clamping a hand over her mouth.

Tuck grinned and wrapped his arms around the man who looked so much like Tuck he had to be his brother Pierce.

The men hugged, slapped each other's backs and then pushed apart.

"You're in a heap of horse dung, brother." Pierce glanced around Tuck at Julia. "You must be Julia." He held out a hand.

Julia took it, her small hand engulfed in his larger one.

"I'm sorry about your sister." Pierce glanced at his brother. "We'll get the bastard, if Tuck and I have anything to do with it."

"Thanks." Julia pulled her hand free, her gaze shifting to the computer on the desktop. The screen displayed the face of a rough-looking character posing for a mug shot.

"Sit." Tuck pressed her into the office chair. "Page

through the images. If one looks remotely like the man you saw, make a note of his name on the pad."

Her hand shaking, Julia clicked a button and another face appeared. For the next fifteen minutes, she searched through what must have been a hundred mug shots, none of which looked remotely like the man she'd seen. The glimpse she'd gotten hadn't given her enough detail to narrow him down to height or hair color. Her head ached and her stomach rumbled.

Tuck and Behling had disappeared, leaving Pierce with her.

"Tough business, losing a family member." Pierce pulled another office chair into the small space and sat beside her. "You and your sister must have been close."

Julia couldn't push a response past the lump lodged in her throat. Instead, she nodded and continued to pore over the blur of faces.

She should be thankful she had this task to keep her mind busy. Searching through an endless array of photographs beat waiting for the phone call from Lily's captors.

"Tuck could get in a lot of trouble for letting you in here when they have an APB out on you." Pierce chuckled. "Sometimes he can be a maverick. It's probably that Lakota blood in us."

Again, Julia didn't respond.

"You must still mean something to him. From what Josh told me, my brother was pretty shook up when he first saw your sister's body—"

Julia shot a glance at the agent. "Shook up?"

Pierce clamped his lips shut. "Sorry. Sometimes I can put my foot in it."

"No, it's okay. Go on." She turned back to the screen, forcing herself to move through the endless sea of faces, her mind racing along, thinking of her daughter, trying to find a killer and listening to what Pierce had to say about Tuck's reaction to what he'd thought was Julia's death.

"Yeah, Tuck assumed it was you lying there. Josh said his face turned white as a sheet. He thought Tuck was going to pass out."

Tuck had been upset by her supposed death?

Pierce snorted. "None of us even knew he was married."

"We had it annulled within two days."

"He never said a word. Not even to our mother."

Julia didn't have anything to say to that. He was probably too embarrassed to tell his family about their crazy mistake, and angry that she'd run out on him without a word. It would take a man as strong and proud as Tuck a long time to get over it and forgive her for being such a coward.

"Anyway, Josh was surprised when he didn't show up the next morning for the helicopter ride back to the branch office. They turned the hotel upside down looking for him. Josh called me to see if I knew what was going on. I was telling Josh to file a missing-person report with the local sheriff when the marina manager came rushing in to report a boat had been stolen."

Out of the corner of her eye, Julia saw a grin flash across Pierce's face. "Sounded like something Tuck would do. Had to have a good reason, too, because while he can be a maverick, as I said, he's usually on the straight and narrow as far as obeying the law."

Julia abandoned her search on the computer and turned to Pierce. "Why are you telling me all this?"

He shrugged, a flush rising up beneath his collar,

spreading across his dark skin. "I'm just saying, Tuck wouldn't have gone to all this trouble if he didn't care."

Julia sucked in a breath and was about to tell Pierce that Tuck cared only because the baby was his. Before she could utter a word, the object of Pierce's storytelling reappeared.

Tuck leaned into the office. "Anything?"

Julia's cheeks heated. Had he heard what she and Pierce had been discussing? Apparently not, or he'd likely be angry.

Tuck set two cups of coffee on the desk.

"Thanks." Pierce reached for one.

"Get your own." Tuck jerked his head to the side. "I'll take it from here. You go spell Josh on standing guard, if you want to be useful."

Pierce nodded. "Just like a Thunder Horse. Send others off to do the dirty work, while you get the pretty girl."

"You're a Thunder Horse," Tuck reminded his brother.

"I know. Wish I'd thought of sending you off first." He stood and stretched. "That's okay. I was digging into the NIGC's records. I need to get back to that anyway. Josh is on his own. You owe him big-time for this."

"I know." Tuck clapped a hand on his brother's back. "Let Mom know I'm okay, will ya?"

Pierce nodded and hurried away, leaving Julia alone with Tuck.

"My brother loading you up with all kinds of lies?" he asked, removing the lid from the coffee cup.

"No." Julia brought another mug shot up on the screen and sighed. "He thinks highly of you."

Tuck shrugged and sipped the coffee before responding. "Saved his butt once or twice."

"You make that sound like nothing." Julia's finger tightened around the mouse. "Agents die every day."

Tuck grinned. "Those weren't Pierce's days."

Julia rounded on him, anger warming the chill of death in her memory. "Death is not a joke. It's final. There's no going back."

"Whoa, sorry. Didn't mean to set off your buttons. You're right. Death isn't a joke. Sometimes we cope by making light of it."

"You don't get it." She turned away from him.

"I do. I lost my best friend in a raid two months ago. I know what it's like to lose someone. It rips your heart out. You second-guess your actions, what you said, what you didn't say. It eats at you until you can't sleep at night."

"Then why do it? Why work for an organization that puts you in the line of fire every day?"

"Someone has to do it."

"That's your reason?"

"Hell, what do you want me to say?" He shoved his hand through his black hair. "I take pride in my country. I want to make it a better place by getting rid of the bad guys."

"What about your family?"

"What I do protects them, as well." Tuck shook his head. "What's your point?"

"What happens when your supervisor has to deliver a message to them that you were killed doing your job?" Julia's lip trembled. She bit down on it to make it stop. When she had a grip on her emotions again, she finished with "What do I tell Lily when someone tells me that you're dead?"

Chapter Eleven

Tuck sat back in his chair, trying to figure out what to say. He'd hoped they could hold off on having this conversation until later. Much later. "I'm sorry you don't approve of my job. But it's who I am."

"You have a daughter now," Julia reminded him. "Doesn't that mean something?"

Hell yeah, Lily meant a great deal to Tuck. She was his baby girl. But did that fact change everything? "Just because I have a daughter now doesn't mean I have to drop the bureau and go to work as an accountant. She's one of the people I'm protecting now by getting the bad guys off the streets."

Julia straightened, her chin tipping up. "Can you guarantee you'll be there for her?"

"Julia, no one can guarantee they'll be there. Life's a crapshoot." He took one of her hands. "I don't plan on dying anytime soon."

"And I don't plan on picking up the pieces of my daughter's broken heart when her daddy doesn't come home." Tears trembled on Julia's eyelashes.

Tuck leaned forward, his eyes narrowing. "What are you saying?"

She looked away. "I'm not so sure it's a good idea for Lily to get to know you."

"What?" Tuck stood up so fast, the wheeled office chair shot backward, hitting the shelf behind it, knocking books over. "I sure as hell *will* get to know my daughter, and she'll know me."

"If you love her, you wouldn't put her through the hell of worrying whether or not you'll come home, of dreading every time the phone rings when you're on assignment. Will she cringe, wondering if this call is the one that announces your death?" Julia turned her back on Tuck and stared at the screen. "Which one of these criminals will take your life? Huh, Tuck? Like they took my father's and my sister's."

Julia hunched over the keyboard, sobs wracking her body.

Tuck's fury melted. Julia had lost two of the people she loved to violent deaths. And from what she'd told him earlier, the death of her father had led to her mother's decline, as well. Tuck couldn't imagine losing his mother or one of his brothers. The loss of his father had been a terrible blow to the entire Thunder Horse clan. He'd been angry at first, blaming everyone and everything. It had all been part of the grieving process Julia was now struggling with.

"Jillian wasn't on assignment—she wasn't murdered because of her job." He grasped Julia's hand and pulled her to her feet, folding her into his arms. "It could have been you instead of her. She was in the wrong place at the wrong time. Lily could have been left motherless if you had been the one taking that video."

"No." Julia shook her head. "I wouldn't have gone after the murderer. Jillian, the FBI special agent, did that. Whatever it is, whatever genetic disposition toward danger you and she have, drove her to investigate. She'd be here today if she'd stayed with me."

Tuck held her, his hand stroking her hair. She had valid points, but that didn't mean she was entirely in the right. "We can't let people get away with murder."

"Why does it have to be you or Jillian or my father?"

"Because we feel it is our responsibility to protect the ones we love."

"And those left behind?" She jerked away from him, eyes blazing through the wash of tears, twin flags of color flying high in her cheeks. "What are we supposed to do, give another sacrificial offering to the greater good and get over it?"

He didn't have an answer for that.

"I remember my mother crying when my father died. She never got over his loss, and eventually she died of a broken heart." Julia gripped the front of his shirt. "Would you wish that on a wife, someone you claim to love? Is that what you want for your daughter's future?"

His heart slipped past a few beats, the knot in his gut tightening. An image of a dark-haired little girl dressed in black standing beside a grave, tears running down her cheeks as she held her mother's hand, flashed through his mind. He sighed. "No. But if we don't identify the killer soon, Lily may not have a future."

Julia stared into his face for a long moment, then disengaged from his embrace and quietly resumed her search through the photos on the database.

"*Wakantanka* is smiling on us," Pierce called out from an office down the hallway.

Julia spun in the chair.

Tuck rose when his brother appeared in the office door. "What did you find?"

"Motive for the NIGC agent's murder." Pierce motioned for Tuck to follow.

"Keep looking," Tuck directed Julia. "I'll be right back." He hurried toward his brother's office.

"There." Pierce jabbed a finger at a screen full of data. "I hacked into Walter Pickett's bank account. Seems a large sum was deposited to his account three days ago and then transferred to an account in the Cayman Islands."

Tuck stared at the screen, studying the figures. "He made that transfer a day before his murder."

"You think maybe whoever murdered him wasn't so happy about that?" Pierce asked. "Which leads to the question, where did he get such a chunk of change?"

Tuck straightened, his eyes narrowing. "Kickback."

"Think we need to have a little talk with the casino manager and see what kind of mischief ol' Walter was up to besides regulating the casino." Pierce grabbed the phone.

Tuck stared at the screen. "Skeeter, in the district office, needs to be working on this. We need to see who owns the Cayman account and where the transfer came from into Walter's account."

"You don't think Walter set it up?"

"I don't want to leave anything to guesswork."

"I'll shoot the info to Skeeter and get him working on the Cayman account."

Tuck nodded. "Good."

"And while you two are out on the town dodging bad guys, I'll see what I can do to arrange a helicopter to get us down to Fort Yates ASAP."

Tuck's lips pressed together. "I'm not so sure it's a good idea for Julia and me to be seen at the airport."

"We'll arrange a safe pickup point. I'll let you know."

"You can't. I'll have to call you when I get another phone. I think someone is monitoring your calls, and that's how they got a trace on my previous phone." He handed the phone to Pierce. "Hide this until I call Josh with my new number. When he passes that number to you, forward my phone to it. Hopefully that way they won't be able to trace Julia and me."

"Will do. If I don't hear from you in the next hour, I'll hop the chopper and head to Fort Yates by myself."

"Sounds like a good backup plan. But I'll be there if at all possible. I just wish we'd hear from Lily's kidnappers."

"They must be lying low until you get that phone from Minneapolis."

"I told them it would take at least five hours to get it back to Bismarck. Thank the spirits. It bought us some time." Tuck pushed a hand through his hair. "I wish they hadn't taken her. Poor Lily doesn't have a clue what's going on. All she'll know is her mother isn't there for her."

Pierce shook his head. "I can't imagine how you feel. That little baby…"

. Tuck inhaled and let it out. "I failed her."

"You didn't. Someone got the jump on you. We'll get her back."

"I hope sooner rather than later—or too late."

Pierce sighed. "Mom's going to be beside herself."

Tuck's eyes widened. "You haven't told her about Lily, have you?"

"No. I didn't want her worrying about her first grandchild yet. She's already worrying enough about you."

Just as Julia had said. "You think Mom wishes we weren't in the FBI?"

Pierce nodded. "I'm sure there are days. But she always encouraged us to follow our hearts and dreams. She'd never hold us back."

"Now that Dad's gone, do you think she'd take it hard if one of us...you know...didn't come home?"

"Yeah. But you know Mom." Pierce smiled. "She'd take comfort knowing we were doing what we were meant to do."

Tuck nodded.

Pierce's brow furrowed. "Why do you ask?"

"Just wondered." Tuck turned on his boot heels. "I'd better get back to Julia."

Pierce caught his arm. "For what it's worth, she's beautiful. I can see why you fell for her."

"Yeah." Tuck shook off his brother's hold and hurried down the hallway and into his office. Julia was beautiful, but he'd fallen for more than just her beauty. She'd been fun and happy. Her gentle, nurturing nature was easy to see through her interaction with others. Now that he'd seen her with Lily, he couldn't imagine being with any other woman.

Julia sat at the desk, paging through mug shots.

"No luck, huh?"

She shook her head. "Not one of these has a white streak at his temple."

Tuck looked over her shoulder as she reviewed yet another image. He wanted to tell her that not every FBI agent died in the line of duty. That he'd be there to walk Lily down the aisle at her wedding. "Julia—"

The phone on the desk buzzed.

Tuck's stomach flipped, a jolt of adrenaline shooting through his veins, his gut telling him this wasn't going to be good news. He lifted the receiver and pressed it to his ear.

"We've got company." Josh's voice was low and urgent.

"Thanks, Josh. We're leaving." He set the receiver

back in its cradle and reached across Julia, clicking out of the screen. "Time to go."

JULIA'S BREATH CAUGHT and held as she leaped to her feet. "Which way?"

"We'll have to time it so we don't cross paths with whoever is coming in the front. We can't be seen by the other agents or my boss. Come on." He grabbed her hand and ran down the hallway to Pierce's office.

Pierce met him at the door. "I know. Josh called." His brother led the way to the stairwell. "Go down the back stairs. I'll head off whoever is on their way up and hold them until you get out."

"Thanks. I'm sorry I got you involved in this."

"I'd have been mad if you hadn't. Family sticks together."

Pierce's words hit Julia like a punch in the gut. The love between the brothers was obvious, and it made her miss her sister even more.

"Be as quiet as you can," Tuck warned her, then pushed through the stairwell door.

Tuck led the way down the steps.

Julia followed, holding on to the rail, easing down the steps, making as little noise as possible. When they reached the bottom, she let go of the breath she'd held all the way down.

Tuck eased the door open and peeked into the hallway. "Can't see anything. Stay here." He slipped through the door. Crouching low, he edged to a corner, peered around and was back in seconds. "Let's go."

Gripping her elbow the same way he'd done when they'd entered the building, he guided her past the guard at the desk, nodding and bidding him a good evening.

Once outside, they power walked to where they'd parked the car a block over.

Once inside, Julia collapsed against the seat, her heart beating so fast she couldn't breathe. "How can you stand all this…this…"

"Danger?" He shrugged. "You get used to it."

Julia couldn't imagine ever getting used to this kind of life. She liked hers neat and orderly, knowing where she should be at each hour of the day. Her heart couldn't take this constant threat for long.

Tuck pulled away from the curb and sped down the backstreets.

When her heartbeat slowed to practically normal, Julia glanced across at Tuck. "What now?"

"We stay away from main thoroughfares and get another prepaid phone. I left my phone with Pierce. I didn't trust that someone hadn't traced it to find us in Hazen. Once I get a new one, we'll call Pierce in a few minutes and have him forward calls from my old phone to this one. That way the kidnappers will be able to reach us, but not trace us." His gaze went to the rearview mirror. "But first we need to ditch the tail behind us."

Julia spun in her seat. A car followed them, its bright lights glaring in her eyes. "How long have they been following us?"

"Since we left the bureau building. Hold on." He gripped the wheel and spun right, turning down a narrow street. His foot jammed onto the accelerator, shooting the car forward. Dodging a parked car that jutted out into the middle of the narrow street, he whipped to the left.

The vehicle behind them made the right turn, just barely missing the parked car, and spun out in a one-eighty rotation trying to make the left turn.

"Hurry! They spun out. You can get the jump on them," Julia shouted.

Tuck goosed the engine, burning rubber on the pavement. At the next road, he jerked the wheel to the left. Buildings were closer together here. Before the other car reached the turn, Tuck spun back to the right. Unless the driver of the other vehicle had seen them make that curve, he wouldn't know which way they had gone.

After another right turn, Tuck raced to the next street and turned right again, heading back in the direction they'd just come on a street two blocks over from the one the vehicle had been following them on.

For the next ten minutes, Julia watched behind them, waiting for the vehicle to reappear from a side road or ram them from the rear.

A wild rush of adrenaline pumped through her veins, setting her nerves on fire. When the danger had passed, she sat back against her seat, her hand pressed to her chest. "Whew!"

"Are you okay?"

Julia looked across at Tuck. "I admit, that was crazy, scary and—" she dragged in a deep breath and let it out in a whoosh "—completely exhilarating." With a grin, she sat up straight, wired and on alert, amazed that she hadn't thought about her sister's death the entire time they'd been eluding their follower.

Tuck chuckled. "You're getting the picture."

"That your job is an adrenaline rush? Yeah, I get that." Her grin faded. "Difference this time is they weren't shooting. You could almost pretend it was a wild roller-coaster ride or a go-kart racetrack."

"Only it's not. One bad turn could have ended it for you and me."

Julia sighed. "I know. With Lily's life on the line,

we can't lose sight of the fact that she still needs parents to raise her."

Tuck sat silently the rest of the ride, pulling into an electronics-store parking lot. "I'll only be a few minutes."

"Hurry." Julia's chest tightened. She didn't like it when Tuck left her. Not after what had happened earlier. "I'll stay out of sight."

"Good girl." He jumped out of the car and entered the building.

Hitting the lock on the door, Julia slid low in her seat, staying out of the beams from the streetlights. Through the glass doors, she could see Tuck moving around the store. Before long he was paying for his purchases and returning to the rental.

"If we had time, I'd switch cars. Whoever was following us now has our license number."

"Should we leave the car somewhere?" Julia asked.

"I don't want to do that to the Glimms—remember, it's rented in their name. We need it to get to the airport. However, we can do the next-best thing."

"And that is?"

He handed her the bag with the phone. "I'll show you. In the meantime, put that thing together and see if it works."

Julia pulled the phone out of the package.

Tuck drove down some smaller residential streets. He pulled into an alley behind an apartment building and stopped. "You should be fine here. I'll be right back."

"Where are you going?"

"Getting a new car."

"What?" She grabbed his arm before he could get out of the car. "You can't steal a car—you're FBI."

"I do what it takes to survive. And I always make it

right in the end." He leaned over and kissed her on the lips. "But I'm not going to steal a car."

Before she could ask him what his plan was, he left the car and pushed through the hedges into the parking lot of the apartment complex.

Two minutes later he was back, carrying a metal license plate.

Julia shook her head. "I should have known." She climbed out of the car and held the screws while he removed them from the old plate and put the *borrowed* plate in its place, using a pocketknife that worked as a screwdriver.

When he finished, he tossed the rental's plate in the trunk and held Julia's door for her. "It's time to call Pierce."

"Why?"

"He's arranging alternate transportation."

"After all the trouble you went through to change the plate on this car?"

"We need all the help we can get where we're headed. More than likely someone is watching Pierce by now."

"Where are we going?"

"Catching a flight to Fort Yates."

All the air left Julia's lungs, and the weight of her sister's death bore down on her heart. "Fort Yates?"

"Need to talk to the casino manager. Seems the NIGC representative, Walter Pickett, was drawing more than his salary to regulate the casino businesses. A *lot* more. We need to find out who was paying him off and who might have wanted to stop that."

Julia huddled in her seat, her body trembling. Going back to Fort Yates would rip her heart into pieces. Jillian was there in the morgue, and Lily wouldn't be at home in her bed in their little apartment. Nothing about Fort Yates would ever be the same.

Once Julia got Lily back, she knew she couldn't stay in Fort Yates any longer than it would take to arrange for Jillian's funeral, pack her belongings and move on.

Fort Yates would never again by the quiet little home she'd established for herself and Lily out in the middle of the North Dakota prairie.

On the tail of that thought was a more urgent one. Would the killer be at Fort Yates still? Just because they had people chasing them didn't mean one of them was the man who'd murdered Jillian. He could be waiting in Fort Yates, directing his minions to do his dirty work.

They could be walking right into the killer's crosshairs.

Chapter Twelve

Tuck agreed to meet his brother at the far end of the airport in a cluster of general aviation hangars. After he'd called Pierce, he made another call to Joseph White Eagle, one of his fishing buddies who lived near Fort Yates, and arranged for him to meet them at the airport. They'd need transportation to the casino. There wasn't a taxi service within fifty miles of Fort Yates.

Careful to watch for trailing vehicles, Tuck pulled into the parking lot of a different hangar than the one Pierce had identified, one over from where he needed to be. He slipped the gray cap over his head and handed Julia the black one. "Keep your head down and do your best to walk like a man."

Julia smiled. "I can't help I've got hips."

"Yes, you do." Tuck's pulse leaped, his groin tightening. Despite the danger—or maybe because of the danger—he found himself more preoccupied by Julia than he should be. Julia's hips and everything female about her had gotten him into trouble in the first place, a year ago. He couldn't afford to be distracted now. "Just don't swing them."

She tucked her long blond hair beneath the hat, pulling it low over her forehead. "Good?"

"Yeah." So good he wanted to kiss her. But right

then, they needed to get a move on. The aircraft would be fueled, preflight check complete and engine revved, waiting on its passengers. They cut through the parking lot to the next hangar.

Pierce had said they should go through the second door from the right of the long building. He'd be waiting for them there.

Tuck located the door and led the way, looking back to ensure Julia followed closely. A car passed on the road nearby, slowing, its headlights glowing ominously until it disappeared around a building. Tuck pressed his back to the side of the structure, pushing Julia behind him, keeping as deep in the shadows as he could get. When the vehicle disappeared past a building, he grabbed Julia's hand. "Hurry."

Julia jogged to keep up.

Once at the door, Tuck pulled it open and stepped inside. As a car passed by from the opposite direction, Tuck snagged Julia's arm and yanked her inside. If he wasn't mistaken, it was the same vehicle that had cruised the road a minute earlier.

He closed the door, letting his eyes adjust to the limited lighting.

"About time, brother." Pierce materialized out of the darkness. "Leon's waiting, engines revved. We have clearance to be the next flight out, if we hurry."

Tuck hooked Julia's arm. "Can you run?"

"It's been a while since track in high school, but I think I can manage."

"Follow right behind me so you don't trip over anything. We didn't want to turn the lights on in the hangar in case someone decided to come and investigate." Pierce took off at a jog, headed for the other end of the building. He slipped through a door out onto the flight line.

A small single-engine Cessna 172 airplane waited on the tarmac, engines roaring, propeller stirring the wind.

"What happened to getting a helicopter?" Tuck yelled without slowing.

"Couldn't. Leon was the only pilot I knew who could get us there and back tonight. It was the Cessna or go by car."

Going by ground would take too long and put them at risk as the only vehicle for a long, straight stretch of highway. They had to go by air.

"We're getting in that?" Julia skidded to a halt beside the craft. The turbulence from the prop whipped her hat off her head, and her hair flew out behind her. "It's no bigger than a crop duster."

"We don't have time to discuss." Tuck opened the door and pointed to the foothold on the wheel strut.

Julia placed her foot on the step and, while Tuck leaned the front seat forward, climbed into the back.

Tuck squeezed in behind her, settling into the tight confines of the tiny craft, his shoulders filling the space. The seats were cracked and stained, and the interior smelled of fish and sweat.

Pierce leaned the front seat back and took the co-pilot's position, settling the headset over his ears. "Hang on!" he shouted.

The plane taxied down the runway, with a few more rattles and a lot more noise than Tuck cared for, picking up speed as it traveled the length of the eight-thousand-feet-long runway.

The craft had to be at least forty years old, patched in some places, paint peeling in others. Tuck held his breath and prayed the little plane could get off the ground fully loaded with four passengers.

Julia sat beside him, her face pale in the lights from the control panel.

He took her hand and squeezed it, their shoulders touching.

Leon pulled back on the throttle and the plane leaped into the air. "Yeehaw!"

Pierce laughed.

Tuck grumbled, finding nothing humorous about a decrepit plane launching into the North Dakota sky on a mission to find a murderer and rescue an infant.

They spun out over Bismarck, making a wide arc before heading south. The trip took only thirty minutes. Conversation was limited to those with headsets, the noise of the engine discouraging any other exchanges, giving Tuck far too much time to think.

Throughout the short flight, Julia held his hand, her fingers curled around his tightly. Tuck couldn't help thinking how right it felt.

Having her so near reminded him of all the reasons he'd fallen for her in the short time they'd spent together a year ago. Even then he'd known what kind of person she was. Her kind and loving beauty had shone like an aura around her. Though their crazy marriage had been a spontaneous, alcohol-inspired decision, Tuck could picture himself with Julia for the long haul.

But how could he convince her to feel the same way? With her fear and aversion to his chosen profession, it would be difficult to win her over to the idea of a life with him. As things stood just now, Tuck would be lucky if Julia even allowed him to spend time with Lily.

His hand tightened around Julia's, his resolve strengthening. Lily was his daughter. No matter how much Julia objected to the FBI, Tuck wouldn't let the little girl grow up thinking her father had abandoned her. And he wouldn't abandon Julia, either. She was part of his life now, and he wouldn't give up until she felt the same way about him.

Pushing aside any anxiety over the upcoming showdown, he focused on the future he wanted, when he'd take Julia and Lily with him to Thunder Horse Ranch. It was where they belonged—especially Lily. She deserved to know her Lakota heritage and her extended family. He smiled as he thought of his mother's reaction to her first grandchild. Lily would be loved.

The Cessna touched down with a jarring thump on the tarmac of the Standing Rock Airport and taxied toward the road leading out. The tiny airport was nothing more than a paved landing strip out in the middle of the prairie. No terminal and no frills whatsoever.

Leon cut the engine, the noise evaporating, the propeller stirring the air as it slowed to a halt.

A beat-up SUV waited on the road—lights off.

Pierce turned to the pilot. "Leon, we need you to stay here and be ready to go at a moment's notice."

Leon nodded. "I'll be here. Got nowhere else to go."

Tuck leaned forward. "We don't know what to expect from our meeting here. But be prepared for anything. Fortunately, you can see us coming a long way off. If all goes well, we'll flash our headlights once. Twice means have the engine ready for immediate takeoff."

"Haven't had this much fun since I raced a polar bear off an icy runway up in Canada. Let me tell you, the bear almost caught me." The pilot clasped his hands together and rested them behind his head. "In the meantime, I'll be catnappin'. Getting too old for these late nights. Danged fishermen and hunters are always pushing for the early-morning hours."

Pierce climbed out and held the seat forward while Tuck unfolded from the back and dropped down to the pavement.

Julia paused at the door, searching for the foothold to get down.

Tuck grabbed her around her waist and lifted her out of the aircraft, setting her on her feet, his hands remaining around her middle for longer than necessary. "Maybe we should leave you with Leon. We don't know how the casino manager will react to our questioning or if the murderer is still here."

Before he finished talking, Julia shook her head. "I'm going. I have the biggest stake in this. Besides, I'm also the only one who actually saw the man who killed the NIGC representative. If I see him here, I can identify him."

Pierce nudged Tuck with his elbow. "She has a point."

Tuck didn't like the idea of Julia being out in the open at the same casino where her sister was shot and killed. His hands rose to Julia's arms. "Well, don't even think you'll be trading yourself to get Lily back. We'll think of something. I don't want you hurt."

She leaned forward and pressed a kiss to his lips. "I'm a big girl. I'll be careful."

Tuck's heart warmed at her fleeting gesture. Still, he didn't want her in the line of fire. "You're not trained in self-defense like we are."

"I'll have *you* there to protect me." She pulled herself up straighter. "I'm going. What we find out here could lead us to the kidnappers. Now, quit arguing. It's wasting what little time we have left."

Tuck hesitated only a moment longer, then grabbed

her hand and led her to the waiting vehicle. "I don't like this. It could get really dangerous without a crowd around to blend into and to keep the killer from making any blatant moves."

"I get that," Julia said. "Let's get in quietly, question our guy and leave before anyone is aware."

Pierce chuckled. "She's sounding more and more like an agent."

Tuck snorted. "Fort Yates is a small town. Everyone is aware of their neighbor's business."

"True, but it's late and most people are in bed." Julia cocked her brows. "I know—I've lived here."

"That might go for the town of Fort Yates, but the casino is a different story." Tuck gave her a pointed look. "I remember."

"In which case, they're too busy gambling to notice." Julia spun toward the car. "If you're done, we should be going."

Tuck grabbed her arm. "Promise me you'll leave all the questioning to me and Pierce."

Her eyes narrowed.

Tuck shook her gently. "Promise, or you're not going."

She sighed. "I promise."

"It's best if you stay in the background. The only reason we're letting you come along is to identify anyone who might look like the killer. Got that?"

Julia heaved another sigh. "Got it." She shook off Tuck's hand and continued toward the SUV.

As the threesome approached, Joseph White Eagle climbed out of the vehicle and held out his hand. The man was pure Lakota, his dark skin, jet-black hair and high cheekbones clearly marking his heritage. "Tuck, good to see you."

Tuck grasped the man's forearm and pulled him into a brief hug. As he stepped back, he motioned to Julia. "This is Julia Anderson."

The man blinked. "I thought you were dead. Then I heard on the news last night your twin sister's body was found on the shore of Lake Oahe and you were a suspect in the killing."

Tuck saved her from responding. "Julia didn't kill her sister. We've been trying to find out who did."

Julia held out her hand to the man, her brows narrowed. "Don't I know you?"

Joseph took her hand and nodded. "You should. My son was in your class a year ago. TJ White Eagle?"

Julia's smile transformed her face from a grieving sister and worried mother to the woman Tuck remembered and fell for. "TJ? I remember him. He was quite an adventurous child."

"That's a nice way of saying he was rowdy." Joe grinned. "You were so patient with him. My wife speaks highly of you still."

"TJ's a nice young man." Her lips twisted. "He just needs a little structure to keep him focused."

Tuck had never heard Julia talk about her teaching job. Even now, with so much riding on this visit to Fort Yates, she displayed a concern for her students that went beyond teaching being just a job.

Tuck's stomach flipped over and he had to remind himself they were on a mission. "Thanks for coming, Joe." Tuck gripped Julia's elbow.

"No problem. Anything for my brothers." Joe inhaled and let it out. "I'm sorry for your loss, Miss Anderson."

Julia nodded, her lips pressing together, tears glistening in her eyes.

Tuck walked her around the side of the car and opened the door for her.

Pierce climbed into the front passenger seat. "Let's go."

Julia scrambled into the backseat, sliding across to make room for Tuck.

As they drove the short distance to the casino, Tuck leaned over the back of the seat in front of him. "You'll need to drop us off close to the casino, but not close enough we can be seen from the building."

Joe nodded. "Gotcha. Lights out?"

"Right. When we get there, we'll slip in the back door." Tuck checked his watch. "It's before midnight, so the manager should still be working. We'll go directly to his office and try to catch him alone."

"And if he's out on the floor?" Pierce asked. "You want me to scope the gaming room first?"

"I can come along and run interference for you," Joe offered.

Tuck shook his head. "I'd hate to get you involved. Two people have already died here."

"I don't mind. I'll just send him to his office for a job application. When he heads that way, I'll hotfoot it back out here and wait in the SUV."

Tuck stared at his friend, his chest swelling. "You're a good man, Joseph White Eagle."

The man shrugged. "You'd do it for me." Just before the turnoff to the casino, Joe turned the vehicle around, heading back the way they'd come, pulled off to the side of the road and parked.

All four passengers got out. Joseph lifted the hood of his vehicle, making it look as though it was stranded. Once the car was situated, they cut cross-country, paralleling the road until they were within one hundred yards of the casino.

Tuck shook his friend's hand. "Give us a few minutes to get in place."

Joe emerged onto the parking lot, wove his way around parked cars and entered through the front door.

Pierce, Tuck and Julia swung wide of the vehicles and the entrance. They approached the casino from the rear, slipping through the door Tuck and Julia had escaped through only a day earlier.

Tuck stopped at the end of a hallway. The manager's office was just around the corner. He remembered it from his previous visit while questioning the man on the deaths of the NIGC rep and Jillian. Had he known what he knew now, he'd have pressed for more answers.

The door was locked. He tapped lightly and waited.

No one answered.

Voices at the end of the hallway alerted him to someone coming. He could hear Joe asking for a job application.

Tuck backed around the corner where Julia and Pierce waited, pressing a finger to his lips. "Shh." He motioned for Pierce to come up alongside him. "I'll go first. We don't want to do this in the hallway." Then he leaned close to Julia's ear. "Stay close behind us and don't interfere," he whispered.

Julia's eyes rounded and she nodded.

Footsteps paused in the corridor and a metal click indicated a door being unlocked.

Tuck peeked down the hall.

Timothy Wilks, the casino manager, was pushing through the open door, balancing a cell phone against his ear, speaking quietly.

Sprinting soundlessly down the corridor, Tuck

sneaked behind the manager and jammed his foot in the door before it closed all the way.

"What the—" The cell phone clattered to the floor and Wilks backed away, his hands held high.

Tuck entered, holding the door open.

"This office is closed for the night." Wilks's voice shook, his face pale.

"Not yet, it isn't." Tuck flipped open his credentials. "You remember me, Special Agent Tuck Thunder Horse, from the other night?"

Wilks shook his head, his eyes narrowing, then nodded. "Oh, yeah, you were one of the FBI agents who came to investigate the murders."

Tuck stepped aside as Pierce entered. "Meet Pierce Thunder Horse, another FBI special agent. We'd like to ask you a few more questions."

"Could it wait until morning?" Wilks looked hopeful.

"No, it can't," Julia said, sliding through the door behind Pierce.

Wilks's face blanched. "M-miss Anderson?"

She nodded.

"I thought you were—"

"Dead?" She pulled the door closed and leaned against it. "Hardly."

"No." The manager's gaze shot from Tuck back to Julia. "I thought you were wanted for the murder of your twin sister."

Julia frowned. "I loved my sister. I would never have hurt her."

The manager pulled a handkerchief from his back pocket and mopped his brow. "I don't know anything more than what I told you before. Why do you need to question me again?"

Tuck closed the distance between them, towering

over the shorter man. "We've learned some surprising details about your NIGC representative, Mr. Pickett. He had a large sum of money deposited in his bank account recently. You wouldn't be paying him a percentage of your profits as a kickback, would you?"

Sweat popped out on Wilks's brow and he mopped it again. "I don't know what you're talking about. We run this casino according to regulations."

"Then you won't mind if we let one of our investigators review your books and operations."

"Go ahead. You won't find anything."

"Because you're dealing under the table." Tuck stepped closer until he stood toe-to-toe with the man, towering over his shorter frame. "If you know anything, you'll tell us. Fraud has a much shorter sentence than murder."

"I didn't murder Mr. Pickett."

"Assuming you didn't kill the rep or Miss Anderson's sister—and for the record, I'm not convinced you didn't do it—accessory to murder carries a higher sentence than fraud, as well."

Wilks backed up another step, bumping into a large wooden desk littered with paper. "I didn't kill anyone." He looked left then right, his face pale and sweaty.

Pierce moved forward to stand beside Tuck. "Who did?"

"I don't know." The manager shook his head, his eyes wide.

Tuck grabbed him by the collar and lifted him until he stood on his toes. "I think you're lying."

"My brother has no patience for liars," Pierce added. "Makes him mad, real mad."

Wilks's hands shook as he clawed at Tuck's grip on his collar. "No, really, I don't know."

"You know more than you're telling us." Tuck pressed his face closer, almost nose to nose with the manager.

"Okay, okay, I paid Pickett a kickback. So what? That doesn't mean I killed him."

"Then who did?" Tuck shook the smaller man.

He yelped. "Maybe it's the man Pickett paid a percentage to."

Tuck shot a glance at Pierce, his attention veering immediately back to the manager. "Now we're getting somewhere." Tuck set the man back on his feet and released his collar. "Who was Pickett paying?"

"He wouldn't tell me. Called him the Big Boss. All I know is the Big Boss isn't around here or even in North Dakota. I think he's out of Minneapolis."

"How do you know?" Pierce asked.

"Pickett let it slip once when the Big Boss's enforcers came to shake us up."

"How'd they shake you up?"

Wilks's shoulders sagged, his gaze darting toward a photograph on his desk. "He threatened to kill me and my family." He looked up, his face haggard. "I got a three-year-old boy and a ten-month-old baby girl. I couldn't let him hurt them."

"I had a baby." Julia stepped forward, tears trickling down her face. "Until they took her."

"Oh, God." Wilks collapsed against his desk, dry sobs shaking his body. "I'm sorry, so sorry. I didn't know it would turn out this way."

Tuck paced across the floor and stopped in front of the manager. "Are there any others involved from Fort Yates?"

"What do you mean?"

"Any law-enforcement officials taking money under

the table? Would they know anything about Pickett's enforcers?"

Wilks shook his head and buried his face in his hands. "Just me." The phone on his desk rang, breaking through the man's anguish. His head came up. "No one calls me at this hour unless there's a problem."

Pierce nodded toward the desk. "Answer it, but don't let anyone know we're here."

"Don't worry. It's probably just a broken machine." The casino manager rounded the desk, lowered himself into his chair and lifted the receiver, his hands shaking so badly he fumbled, almost dropping it. "Wilks." He listened, his gaze going to Tuck. "Thanks." He dropped the phone on the desk. "You have to get out."

"Why?"

"Get out now!" He rose to his feet, waving his hands. "They're coming."

Julia took a step toward Wilks. "Who?"

"They know," Wilks mumbled, coming around the desk. "Somehow they know."

Tuck grabbed Wilks by the collar again. "Who's coming?"

The man stared into Tuck's eyes, his own expression desperate, terrified. "The enforcers."

Chapter Thirteen

Julia turned so fast she stumbled over her own feet. She caught herself before she fell, and raced for the door.

Tuck beat her to it. "No, wait." He opened it carefully and peered out. "It's clear. Julia, follow me. Wilks next and Pierce bring up the rear."

Tuck stepped into the hall.

Julia took a deep breath and rushed after him. When she looked back for Wilks, he stood at the door to his office, unmoving.

"Come on," Julia entreated.

He shook his head. "I can't. They'll go after my family." The manager stepped aside and waved Pierce through. "Go on. I'll cover for you somehow. Just leave before they see you with me."

Pierce slipped by Wilks and urged Julia forward. "Move it."

"What about Wilks?" Julia ground to a halt.

Pierce ran into her. "Don't stop. We have to keep going."

She shook her head. "We can't leave him. They'll kill him."

Tuck grabbed her hand and leaned close. "It's his choice. You have to think about Lily. Focus on getting her back."

"But he'll die." Julia edged forward reluctantly.

"We don't know that. But we do know we have to get that phone with the video to the kidnappers by midnight. If we don't—"

"Don't say it. Don't even think it. Lily is going to be okay. We're going to get her back." Julia nodded at Tuck. "Don't just stand there. Move."

Tuck spun and sprinted for the back door. When he got there, he ducked through first.

Pierce grabbed her arms to keep Julia from exiting. "Stay here until we motion you to follow."

Julia huddled close to the floor, carefully keeping out of sight, her heart pounding, watching for their signal while listening for footsteps in the hallway behind her.

The brothers split and went in opposite directions, disappearing into the night.

Julia rocked back and forth, pressing her knuckles to her lips to keep from crying. Now was not the time to give in to tears.

A shout echoed through the corridor and footsteps pounded toward her.

Julia jumped to her feet and pushed through the door, running in the direction Tuck had gone.

Darkness surrounded her in the shadow of the structure. She could barely see three feet in front of her. She brushed her hands against the structure, racing toward the corner where moonlight lit the adjacent side.

When she'd almost reached the corner, she ran into a wall of muscle and bounced back.

A hand grabbed her arm, spun her around and clamped a hand to her mouth so fast she didn't have time to scream.

"Shh. It's me," Tuck said into her ear, his hand dropping to her shoulders.

Julia sagged against him.

"They're all over the front and working their way back here. We have to swing wide of the building."

"What about Pierce?"

"He'll know to make for the SUV."

She nodded, sucking air into her lungs, willing her speeding heart to slow.

Tuck peered around the side. "Move fast and stay low." Keeping in the shadows for as long as he could, he ran away from the back of the building, in the opposite direction of the highway and their getaway car.

Julia sprinted to keep up with the Lakotan. When she thought he'd keep running all the way to Minnesota, he turned south and ran some more.

Her lungs hurt and her calves burned, but Julia forced herself to keep going. With every footfall, she thought *Lily.*

No matter how tired or how much pain she was in, she had to keep going for her daughter.

Finally, they arrived at the highway where the SUV had been parked. It was nowhere to be seen.

Julia's heart dropped to her belly and she doubled over in an effort to breathe without sobbing. "Oh, God, where are they?"

"I don't know, but Joe wouldn't leave without a good reason." Tuck hooked her arm and pulled her off the road, heading south toward the airport.

Before they'd gone a hundred yards, the hum of an engine edged toward them.

Tuck dropped to the ground, dragging Julia with him. They waited as the vehicle neared where they crouched in the dirt.

Julia strained to make out the shape and size, her

heart leaping when she recognized the SUV as Joseph White Eagle's.

Tuck laid a hand on her shoulder, urging her to stay put. He rose and stepped into the road.

A window rolled down and Joe stuck his head out. "Tuck? Thank the spirits. *Wakantanka* must be looking out for you. Get in."

Julia staggered to her feet and fell into the backseat, grateful for the respite from the cross-country run.

Tuck slid in next to her.

Pierce grinned over the back of the passenger seat. "About time you two made it here."

Joe took off with the headlights turned off, racing down the highway. Clouds skittered across the sky, giving them bouts of limited visibility.

Hanging on to the armrest, Julia swallowed her fear and tried to think happy thoughts to keep from screaming at every shadow that seemed to pop up out of the road.

Tuck slipped her free hand in his and held on. "It's going to be okay."

"Is that a promise?" She glared at him, anger replacing fear, exhaustion adding fuel to the fire inside. "And can you promise we'll get Lily back safely?"

He let go of her hand and turned away. "I can't promise anything. I can only do the best I can."

Julia regretted her outburst almost as soon as she'd let loose. She missed the warmth of his hand holding hers.

Tuck didn't turn her way, refusing to meet her gaze.

Leaning back against the seat, Julia closed her eyes and tried to remember the last time she'd been rested, unafraid and normal.

"Uh-oh," Joe said from the front seat. "We got company."

Heart leaping into her throat, Julia sat up, her gaze going to Joe, who was looking into the rearview mirror.

He hit the accelerator, goosing the SUV forward, urging it to go faster.

Julia spun in her seat to glance behind them.

"There are two sets of headlights closing in fast." Tuck turned to Joe. "How far to the airport?"

"Two minutes at this speed."

"Use the lights. They already know we're here."

Joe flipped the switch, illuminating the road in front of them. He increased the speed even more.

Julia's breath caught and held, the roadside blowing past her in a dark blur. The vehicles behind them were still just bright specks of light in the distance, but the lights were getting bigger.

Hurry, she urged silently.

As they neared the turnoff for the Standing Rock Airport, Julia gripped the armrest, holding on for dear life.

Joe took the turn going too fast. The SUV fishtailed, spinning out on loose gravel.

Gripping the steering wheel so tightly his knuckles turned white, Joe righted the vehicle and sped on.

"Flash the headlights twice!" Tuck yelled.

The headlights blinked on and off, and on and off again.

An answering blink flashed from the tarmac ahead.

"When we stop, get out and run for the plane," Tuck told Julia. "Don't bother looking behind you. It will only slow you down."

Julia glanced back one more time, then concentrated on the task ahead. She reached out and grabbed Tuck's hand and squeezed it hard. "Be careful, will ya. needs a daddy."

"Even if he's FBI?" Tuck stared across the seat at her.

Before Julia could answer, the SUV skidded to a stop, five feet from the plane.

The plane's turboprop engine roared and the propeller spun, kicking up dust and debris.

Julia shoved her door open, scrambled out of the SUV and raced for the plane.

Pierce beat her there and folded the front seat forward. Before her feet could find the footholds, hands lifted her from behind and pushed her inside. She fell on the floor and crawled out of the way as Tuck tumbled in behind her.

Pierce jumped in and slammed the door, and the plane lurched forward on the tarmac.

Julia pulled herself up in the seat and glanced out the narrow window.

Joe had turned his SUV around and was racing back the way they had come, heading straight for the two pairs of headlights aimed at him.

At the last minute, both vehicles split and Joe's SUV sped between them, speeding toward the highway.

Pressing a hand to her chest, Julia dared to breathe, praying Joe would be all right.

The two vehicles spun out onto the tarmac and chased the plane as it lumbered across the uneven asphalt, gathering speed.

"Hurry," Julia muttered. "Hurry."

The SUVs were less than thirty yards behind them when the plane left the ground and soared into the air.

Julia almost laughed with relief until she heard the dull thunk, thunk of metal hitting metal.

Tuck doubled over, grabbing for his right calf and swearing a blue streak.

"What's wrong?" Julia leaned over him and gasped.

Bright red fluid coated his hand and dripped onto the cabin floor.

"They're shooting at us," Tuck said, his words strained between clenched teeth. "Get us over the lake, quick."

"Can't until we get a little higher."

Another thunk blasted up through the front. Shards of glass and plastic splintered outward.

"Damn! They hit the control panel!" Leon shouted above the engine noise, then leaned forward, tapping on the gauges, his gaze shooting side to side. "It's shorted out more than half of the instruments."

Even Julia, in the backseat with the engine noise loud enough to inhibit her hearing, heard Leon's words. Her stomach fell back to the earth. No instruments? What did that mean? Whatever it meant, it had to be bad for Leon to be so freaked out.

Pierce laid a hand on Leon's arm. "We can do this."

"What? Fly at night without instruments? Are you crazy?" Leon glared at Pierce, his glance shifting to the windows.

"Are we still in the air?" Pierce looked down.

Leon did the same.

Julia glanced out the window. The ground was getting farther and farther away. The SUVs carrying the men who'd shot at them were nothing but dots of light now.

"We're still climbing." Leon sucked in a deep breath and let it out slowly.

"We can't go back and land at Standing Rock Airport." Tuck leaned forward, speaking in the same calm, even tone loud enough for the nervous pilot to hear. "It's only thirty minutes to Bismarck. You can do it, Leon."

Leon rolled his shoulders and nodded. "You bet your badges I can. I've flown in much worse weather conditions. Granted, I wasn't being shot at."

He gripped the yoke and tested the foot pedals. "I still have the turn coordinator, and the plane responds to the yoke." Leon nodded again. "The moon's rising, the clouds are clearing, so we have plenty of light to check ground references. We can fly this plane without any stinkin' instruments." The pilot leaned his head back and shouted, "Yeehaw!" The plane veered toward the heavens and Leon focused, bringing the craft back level with the earth.

Julia's stomach turned over. She didn't know anything about flying an airplane, but a limited number of working instruments sounded pretty serious. Flying without them at night could end up deadly. Yet if Leon, Pierce and Tuck thought they could do it, she'd have faith that they knew what they were talking about.

"Look!" Tuck pointed out the window to the airport they'd left behind.

Flashing red and blue lights blinked like toys on the highway below. Two law-enforcement vehicles sped toward the airport, blocking the only road out. The dark SUVs veered off the runway and went off-road, their lights jerking up and down as they bumped across uneven terrain.

"Guess the sheriff got wind of something," Tuck said.

"Maybe Wilks placed the call, his conscience getting the better of him." Julia watched until the specks of light grew too small to pick out of the landscape. She leaned back in her seat, barely able to relax, knowing they still had many miles to cover before they reached

Bismarck. If the plane crash-landed, they might miss their meeting time to make the exchange for Lily.

Her pulse continued to beat erratically, her foot tapping the floor.

Tuck sat forward on his seat and pulled the hem of his shirt from his trousers. He poked a knife into the fabric and ripped off a long swatch.

Julia clapped a hand to her mouth, just remembering Tuck had been hit by one of the bullets. "Let me." She scooted off the seat and sat on the floor beside him, peering at the injury in the moonlight shining through the little window.

Tuck turned so that she could see the gash. "It's just a flesh wound, but I didn't want to bleed all over Leon's fine flying machine."

Leon snorted. "Like I don't get enough game blood and fish guts spilled in here. You aren't going to hurt it."

Julia cringed at the thought of old fish guts and blood infecting Tuck's wound. "Let me see that knife."

Tuck dug in his pocket and pulled out the small folding knife he'd used on his shirt.

Careful not to injure him further, Julia cut away the pant leg from Tuck's knee down to his ankle.

Pierce tapped her on her shoulder with a fresh bottle of water. "Use this to clean it."

She opened the cap and poured the water over the gash. Once the blood was cleaned away, Julia let out the breath she'd been holding. "You're right. It's just a flesh wound. Are you up-to-date on your tetanus shot?"

Tuck grinned. "Yes, ma'am."

With the swatch of fabric, Julia wrapped the calf, knotting the ends over the gash for added pressure to stanch the blood flow. When she was done, she glanced up into Tuck's incredibly black eyes. Her heart skipped several beats before galloping as fast as it had when she'd been running full tilt.

"Thanks." He held out his hand and pulled her into the seat beside him, his arm draped over her shoulder as if it belonged there.

Julia didn't ask him to remove it. After all they'd been through, his arm around her felt good—safe. She leaned against him. "What time is it?"

Tuck pulled his sleeve up. "Ten-thirty."

"Think they have the phone and video back from Minneapolis by now?"

"Let's hope so."

"I have to be ready to take it to them when they call."

His arm tightened around her shoulders. "No. If you take it, they'll kill you as the only other eyewitness to the crime."

"I need to be there for Lily."

"She'll need you alive."

"Didn't they specifically say I had to bring it?"

"They did, but you're not going." His jaw was set tight, his gaze unwavering.

"Then who will take it?" Julia asked.

"I'll make the exchange."

Julia leaned away from him so that she could look directly into his face, her hand resting on his chest. "And your life is any less important than mine?"

Tuck ran a finger down the side of her cheek. "Lily needs her mother. Yours is the only familiar voice and face to her."

Julia captured Tuck's fingers and pressed them to her face. "She's going to know yours, too."

"You're sure? Less than twenty-four hours ago, you weren't. I work for the FBI. That's not going to change."

Julia nodded. "I know. She deserves to know how hard you work and how brave you are."

"And if I die in the line of duty?"

Swallowing hard, Julia forced words past her suddenly constricted throat. "She won't be happy, but I'll help her to understand that you gave your life doing what you felt was right. Making it a better place for her to live." She'd help her daughter understand why her daddy wouldn't come to see her anymore, but who would help Julia deal with a world without Tuck Thunder Horse?

When tears welled in her eyes, she fought to keep them from falling. She'd cried enough for a lifetime. It was time she toughened up like her sister.

The scattered lights below grew closer together as the plane neared Bismarck.

Leon rummaged through a satchel on the floor beside him and unearthed a handheld radio. He switched it on and gave his call sign. "Bismarck Approach, inbound with partial panel failure."

The radio squawked and the tower responded. "Are you declaring an emergency?"

"Not at this time," Leon responded.

After a short pause from the air-traffic controller, he returned with, "You are clear to land on runway One-three."

Bright landing lights guided them to the runway.

As Leon maneuvered the craft closer to the ground, Julia held her breath, her hand gripping Tuck's thigh, fingernails digging in. She felt as if they were speeding toward death, moving much too fast to land safely.

Tuck's hand covered hers.

A calm settled over Julia, her heartbeat returning to

something resembling normal by the time the tires hit the tarmac with a gentle bump.

She wanted to cheer, to celebrate living through another brush with death, but she couldn't until her baby was safely back in her arms.

Leon taxied to the hangar and brought the plane to a complete stop. "You guys go. I'll file the report. You can add to my statement when you've got everything settled. Now go."

Pierce shook Leon's hand and climbed down, shoving the seat forward for Tuck and Julia to get out.

Tuck patted Leon's back, then jumped to the ground.

Julia leaned over the back of the seat and placed a kiss on Leon's startled face. "Thanks." Then she slid across the backseat and stood in the doorway.

"Hey, what's with the kiss?" Tuck held out his hands, caught her around the waist and swung her to the tarmac and into his arms.

Julia leaned up on her toes and pressed a kiss to Tuck's lips. She'd meant it to be a brush of the mouth.

Tuck's arms tightened around her, crushing her against him, his mouth consuming her in a mindblowing kiss.

When he set her back on her feet, she felt lightheaded and off balance. She leaned on him until she was steady.

"If you two are through smoochin', we need to get back to the office and see if the phone made it back from Minneapolis." Pierce walked away as if he meant them to fall in step behind him.

Tuck stared down at her a moment longer, then he skimmed her forehead with a soft kiss. "Come on, we have a baby to bring home." He grabbed her hand and hurried after Pierce.

Julia's heart squeezed in her chest. How could she be thinking about Tuck when her baby was missing? Her thoughts had grown so confusing, she didn't know what she wanted anymore.

Crystal clear in her mind was the determination to bring Lily home safe. What would happen between her and Tuck after that? She'd have to cross that bridge when she got there.

Tuck led them back to the rental car, limping slightly on his injured leg.

Pierce opened the back door and Julia came to a halt beside him. "Tuck, you should sit up front, but let Pierce drive."

"Don't you want Tuck to sit with you?" Pierce asked.

She shook her head. "You two are the FBI agents. Talk. We need a plan." She slid into the backseat and smiled up at Tuck's brother. "I need you two focused. I want Lily back."

Pierce nodded and climbed into the driver's seat. "Smart as well as beautiful."

"I know." Tuck slid into the passenger seat.

Pierce backed out of the parking space.

Tuck dialed the office and waited for Behling to pick up. "Behling?"

Julia leaned forward, trying to hear Behling's response, but couldn't.

"It did?" Tuck glanced back at Julia, giving her a thumbs-up.

Julia pressed a hand to her chest. They had the phone. Now they could exchange it for Lily.

Tuck's brows furrowed. "What? You didn't, did you?"

As quickly as the hope rose, it died, and Julia waited,

her breath lodged in her lungs, for Tuck to give her the bad news she was sure would come.

"We'll be there soon to collect." Tuck clicked the off button and turned to Pierce. "The supervisor from Minneapolis has been in the office since we left, demanding answers for the death of one of his agents."

"Don't worry about him." Pierce's lips thinned. "We'll give them to him when we have them."

"He's still there. We have to get past him to get the phone."

"So we get past him." Pierce shot a glance at his brother. "You can't make the trade for Lily without it."

"He knows Julia's on the run with me. He wants her brought in along with the phone and video."

Pierce slammed his palm against the steering wheel. The car swerved to the right before he corrected. "Who the hell told him about the phone?"

Tuck shook his head. "I don't know."

Julia leaned over the back of the seat, bile rising in her throat, her stomach roiling. "Did Behling give him the phone?"

Tuck gave her a thin smile. "No. He intercepted the delivery before the supervisor saw it come in."

Julia sank back against her seat, nauseous and weak. "We can't let him have it. Lily's life depends on it."

"Behling will keep it safe." Tuck glanced back at her.

She held his gaze for a brief moment, the icky feeling passing. Tuck was her rock in this disaster. He'd get her and Lily through. Julia had to believe it—she had no one else.

Chapter Fourteen

Tuck took the circuitous route to the FBI building in downtown Bismarck to avoid any potential followers—but he couldn't help but chafe at the wasted time. The clock on the dash glared a bright green, reinforcing the need for them to hurry. With only an hour left before the designated exchange, they couldn't afford to lose even a minute.

Pierce glanced back at Julia as Tuck parked the vehicle a block from the building near a large trash bin. "Tuck and I will go in. You stay in the car and keep low."

Tuck knew the announcement wouldn't make Julia happy and he'd be worried about her the whole time, but leaving her with the car was for the best.

Julia unbuckled her belt and scooted toward the door. "I want to go in with you."

Tuck shook his head and glanced at her in the mirror. "We barely got you in and out last time. It's too risky to do it again. Especially with the regional director breathing down our necks."

Julia chewed her lip and finally nodded. "Fine. But leave the keys in case we need to make a quick getaway."

Pierce's brows rose as a grin spread across his face. "I told you she'd make a good agent."

Julia frowned. "Just hurry. I don't want the kidnappers to have any reason to hurt Lily."

"We're out of here." Tuck jumped out of the front seat and opened the back door for Julia to get out. "Sit up front, and remember to stay low. The keys are in the ignition."

As she stood, he pulled her into his arms and kissed her soundly, then set her away from him, his heart pounding. "You know we have to talk when this is all over."

She nodded and ducked beneath his arm to slide into the driver's seat. "Get that phone."

Tuck took off at a run toward the FBI building, wincing each time his foot hit the ground, pain shooting through his leg from the bullet wound.

Pierce fell in behind him. "How are you going to explain your torn pants?"

"Just go in front of me past the front desk and avoid everyone."

"Gotcha." Pierce took the lead as they entered the front door of the FBI satellite-office building. He nodded to the guard on duty, flashed his credentials and moved on.

Close behind him, Tuck did the same, trying to walk without a limp to keep from drawing attention.

They took the stairs to avoid meeting anyone getting on or off the elevator and traveled up to the floor where Josh's office was located.

Tuck pushed through the stairwell door and listened. Loud, angry voices came from the direction of his supervisor's office. He hurried toward Josh's office, keeping low and moving fast, ignoring the dull ache spreading through his bad leg.

Josh sat at his desk, his fingers drumming the arm of his chair, his gaze glued to the telephone.

Tuck slipped in behind him and laid a hand on his shoulder.

His friend jumped, his eyes wide until he recognized Tuck. He blew out a long breath and sagged back into his chair. "Thank goodness you're here."

"What's happening?"

"Supervisory Special Agent-with-an-attitude Ray Mullins is grilling our boss over the Fort Yates case." Josh pointed at Tuck. "You need to get out of here. I heard your name come up several times."

"What else have you heard?"

"Mullins wants the girl and the phone."

Tuck frowned. "How does he know about the phone? The only ones who might know about it are the kidnappers and us." Tuck waved a hand at the three of them.

Josh shrugged. "I haven't breathed a word. I don't know how he got that information."

"You think Skeeter told him?" Tuck asked Pierce.

Pierce shook his head. "Skeeter works in the Minneapolis office, but I told him it was highly sensitive and he shouldn't let anyone know what it is or that he's even working it."

"Even his supervisor?"

Pierce nodded. "Even his supervisor. My connection can be trusted."

Josh cocked his head. "It's quiet. That can't be good." He dug in a file-cabinet drawer beneath his desk and surfaced with a package, the seal unbroken. "Take it and leave."

Tuck snatched the package from Josh's hand. "Thanks,

man, I owe you." He turned to duck out the door of Josh's office.

Pierce slammed a hand to his chest. "Wait."

Footsteps pounded the floor, headed their way.

"I'll handle this. You wait until the coast is clear."

"Let me," Josh whispered.

"You've done enough. Besides, I want to see what this guy knows and why. And after I lose him, I need to place a call to Skeeter." Pierce stared at his brother. "Be careful and call me when you hear from the kidnappers."

Tuck nodded and hung back, quietly tearing the phone from its packaging. It looked just as it did when he'd handed it over to his brother, what felt like a long time ago.

Pierce hurried down the hallway. "You must be Supervisory Agent Mullins. Pierce Thunder Horse. Behling tells me you lost an agent?"

After a minute or two, Pierce led the supervisor away, their voices fading.

Josh stepped out into the hallway and stretched. "All clear. You can make it to the stairwell."

Tuck slipped the damaged phone into his back pocket and ran for the stairwell, careful to keep his steps from ringing out through the corridors. He took the stairs two at a time, arriving at the bottom out of breath and with a fiery pain running all the way up his leg, but determined to get out and take the call from the kidnappers. Without Pierce to block the guard's view, he just moved past quickly, giving a friendly wave, pushing through the door out into the street.

A car was parked illegally across from the door, the windows too dark to see inside.

Tuck ducked his head and turned left, hurrying away

from the building while watching the suspicious car through his peripheral vision.

When the door opened and a man got out, Tuck didn't wait around to see if he was friend or foe. He took off at an all-out sprint.

As he reached the corner of the building, he heard a soft popping sound, like that made by a gun with a silencer, then something hit his arm, spinning him around.

He regained his footing and ducked low.

Another pop nicked the wall beside him, spitting chunks of concrete and dust into the air.

Tuck slipped around the corner and ran as fast as he could, slipping between the buildings to the street a block over. He didn't want to put Julia in danger, but he had to get to her with the phone.

With footsteps pounding against the pavement behind him, Tuck couldn't go directly to where she waited in the car. He zigzagged through buildings, leading his pursuer away from Julia and the car. Then he cut back, moving more quietly, sticking to the shadows until he reached the huge trash container.

The car sat where he'd left it, the driver's seat appearing empty, until a head popped up over the steering wheel.

Julia's eyes widened and her mouth formed an O.

Tuck stepped out of the shadows.

Her immediate smile of relief made him glad to be alive. She punched the button releasing the door lock and climbed across the console to the passenger seat.

Tuck slung the driver's door open and jumped in, turning the key in the ignition and shifting into Drive almost immediately. He spun out onto the road and floored the accelerator.

A figure emerged out of a side street and ran out into the middle of the road, blocking their path.

"Duck!" Tuck yelled and drove straight for the man in the road. At the last moment, he slid down behind the dash.

Julia bent down as the window shattered, spraying glass all over the interior of the car.

Tuck's head came up almost immediately. He hadn't run into the guy so he must have jumped clear of their oncoming car right after shooting at the windshield. A glance in the rearview mirror confirmed it.

The man rolled to his feet and took aim again.

Julia picked that moment to lift her head.

Tuck planted a hand on the back of her neck and shoved her back down. "Stay down!"

The back window exploded in a shower of glass.

Tuck leaned to the left, trying to find a good angle to look out the shattered windshield without making himself a target to the shooter behind them.

At the next corner, Tuck turned right so sharply the car jumped up onto the curb. He fought to bring it under control, riding along the sidewalk for several yards before the wheels bumped down on the pavement.

"Oh, my God, you've been hit!" Julia jerked up in her seat, her hand going out to his arm.

"It's nothing."

"You're still bleeding." She tried to touch it.

"Leave it," he barked, glancing in the side mirror. The rearview mirror was useless, reflecting nothing but the broken shards of the rear window. "I need that arm to drive. We've got bigger problems." He couldn't keep driving the little rental car with all its damage. Even if he could figure out how to see well enough to drive safely, they'd be far too conspicuous.

The vehicle he'd seen sitting in front of the FBI building had taken the corner and was closing in fast.

"Stay low and hold on," he said.

Julia reached for the seat belt, buckling it around herself before she bent over. "Who would be shooting at us? It doesn't make sense for them to use Lily as a hostage if they shoot me first."

Tuck's stomach sank with the truth. "They aren't going to leave any live witnesses." He gritted his teeth and swung left onto the next street.

The vehicle behind him kept coming, relentless and gaining ground.

With limited visibility, he couldn't outrun the men chasing them. He had to do something quickly.

He slammed the pedal to the floor and shot straight toward the busiest section of town with the most traffic lights and cars, even at this time of night.

As they approached an intersection, the light flashed red. Cars moving perpendicular from them entered the intersection from both sides.

Julia looked up and yelped. "Are you crazy? Stop!"

Tuck jammed the accelerator to the floor, slipping between an SUV and a truck, barely missing the SUV and nicking the bumper of the pickup.

Horns blared and vehicles slammed to a standstill in the intersection behind him. The car that had been following skidded sideways and broadsided the pickup, further tangling the traffic. It tried to back out, but another vehicle blocked its path.

Tuck dragged in a shaky breath and turned at the next corner. "I can't see. We have to get a different vehicle."

"How, without using your credit card?"

"I have one at my apartment here in town."

"Won't they be watching?"

"Not if they're stuck in a traffic jam." He hoped. "We should hear from the kidnapper soon."

Tuck took the shortest route to his apartment, choosing to hide the damaged rental car a block away, as he had at the FBI building. If trouble awaited, he wanted to spot it before it caught him.

He pulled in front of a deserted house with an untrimmed tree hanging low over the side yard. Shifting into Reverse, he opened his door and guided the car beneath the branches.

When he had the vehicle hidden, he turned off the engine. "You know the drill. Stay here and stay low until I drive by with the car. I'll flash the lights to let you know it's me."

Julia reached for the wound on his arm and sighed. "Do something about this while you're in your apartment."

He cupped her face and leaned close. "Thanks for being such a trooper."

She sniffed, a single tear rolling across her cheek. "I'm not. You're the one taking all the hits."

"All for a good cause, baby." He kissed her, his lips laying an unmistakable claim on hers, his tongue pushing past her teeth to sweep across hers in a slow, gentle glide. He wanted to keep on kissing her, but he had to get another vehicle, and quickly. The call should be coming through in the next ten minutes.

He handed the prepaid phone to Julia, knowing the kidnappers would want her to be the one to take the call. "If the kidnappers call while I'm in my apartment, don't do anything crazy. Don't let them know where you are, and don't go off without me. It won't end well for you or Lily if *you* show up for the exchange." He pulled the damaged cell phone from his back pocket and laid that in her palm, as well. "If for some reason I'm not back in ten minutes, call Pierce and let him conduct the exchange." He opened his door and had one foot on the pavement when Julia caught his arm.

"Everything will be all right. I know it will. Oh, and take a minute to wash your wounds."

He shook his head. "No time for that."

"Yes, there is. Don't worry about me. I'll make sure it all works out. And when this is over, we'll have that talk." She pulled him close and kissed him quickly.

Tuck got out.

Julia slipped into the driver's seat and nodded at him. "Go."

He didn't want to leave her. "Lock the doors."

She looked down and pushed a button, and the locks snicked into place.

Time pressing him forward, Tuck left the car and jogged to the line of bushes edging the parking lot of his apartment. With one last glance at the drooping tree that effectively hid the car, he dug his keys from his pocket, slipped through the bushes and scanned the parking lot for any cars he didn't recognize. Nothing looked suspicious, but he knew looks could be deceiving.

Keeping to the shadows, he angled his way to the staircase and climbed to the second floor, easing up to his apartment door.

It hung open, the jamb splintered. Someone had broken in. Was that someone inside waiting for him to return?

JULIA STRAINED TO SEE into the darkness, fear mounting with each passing minute. She stared down at the phone in her hand, willing it to ring and yet dreading what would happen when it did. If Tuck was there, she'd handle it better. Alone, she'd fumble, maybe saying something that would get herself—or Lily—killed.

She rocked back and forth, her stomach knotted so tightly it hurt. How long had it been since she'd eaten? Hours? Days? How could anyone eat when her child was missing, maybe hurt, probably crying?

Her chest tightening, Julia let out a low moan. "Please, please, please be okay." She closed her eyes and sent a silent prayer to the heavens to bring her baby back safely.

The few hours since she'd been taken felt like weeks, a lot happening in that short time frame.

One thing stood out above it all. Tuck.

He'd been there every step of the way, saving her from one bad situation after another, holding and encouraging her when she didn't think she could go another step. He came up with solutions to seemingly impossible problems.

Without him, she'd be lying dead somewhere, just like Jillian. A sob rose up her throat, and she fought hard to swallow it down. Jillian wouldn't have dissolved into hysteria, wouldn't have cried herself into a useless mess. She'd have stood up for what was right, saved those who couldn't save themselves and risked her life so that innocents wouldn't suffer.

Her sister had loved her job and so had her father. On more than one occasion Jillian had said she liked being a part of something that was bigger than just herself. An organization that made a difference in people's lives, that made the world a safer place.

Pretty much what Tuck had told her. How could Julia expect him to give up something he loved so much that it had become a part of him? It made him the man he was, strong, smart, caring and willing to risk his life to save her and Lily's.

Even before he'd left her in the car to go to his apartment, Julia had known deep down that she couldn't let him put himself at risk to make the exchange for Lily. The kidnappers might know by now that Lily was Tuck's daughter. If they had that information, they'd use it against him. Tuck wasn't the right man to make the exchange.

She remembered that Jillian's supervisor was at the FBI building. Granted, Jillian had said not to trust anyone, even the FBI, but if she was worried about corruption in the local FBI office then surely that didn't include her supervisor, who was from another state entirely.

The phone in her hand rang.

Julia's fingers jerked away as if the device was a striking snake. The phone fell down the crevice beside the seat, still ringing.

It could be the kidnappers.

Horrified at the thought of missing the call, Julia dug her hand between the seats, the phone just out of reach. She dropped to the floor, shards of glass pushing through her jeans, tearing at her knees. Her hands felt beneath the seat for the cool-metal-and-plastic phone. When she found it, her fingers curled around it, her heart skittering through her chest.

Kneeling on the floor, she pulled the phone from beneath the seat. "Blocked Sender." Julia jabbed at the talk button.

"Where's my baby?" she sobbed into the phone.

The voice spit out an address so fast Julia almost didn't catch it all. "Be there in fifteen minutes or the baby dies."

"How do I know she's still alive?" Julia demanded.

A pause ensued, then the distinct sound of a baby's cry could be heard through the receiver.

Julia's grip tightened on the phone, and she jammed it against her ear. "Lily?"

"Be there. Alone." The click shut off the lifeline between Lily and Julia, ripping her heart right out of her chest.

For a moment Julia sat staring at the seat in front of her, unseeing through the flood of tears filling her eyes. Then a glance down at the time indicated on the phone's display shook her out of the trance and spurred her to action. Tuck would be back at any moment.

She looked back through the recent calls and selected one in particular. Hitting Redial, she made the call. When she'd finished, she knew what she had to do.

She pushed open the car door and climbed out.

Tuck had done enough. It was time she did something for him, like getting Lily back without putting Tuck in danger again.

Chapter Fifteen

Tuck glanced around at the parking lot below his apartment, searching once more for movement. Then he gently nudged his door open with the tip of his toe. It swung inward on silent hinges.

The triangular beam shining in from the streetlight cast a soft blue glow into the living room. Tuck studied the space, shock quickly replaced by anger at the amount of damage. The couch had been tipped over, cushions ripped, his glass coffee table shattered and books strewn. Anything that could be broken lay shattered on the floor.

Tuck moved from room to room, careful not to make a noise. It didn't take him long to determine that the apartment was empty. With only a few minutes to spare, he ripped off his shirt and jeans, leaving them lying on the floor. What difference did it make? He could clean up when they had Lily back.

A quick douse in a cold shower to rinse off the blood, a haphazard job of bandaging, and he was dragging on clean jeans over his wet body. After slipping into tennis shoes, he grabbed a shirt from his drawer, a jacket from his closet and the SIG Sauer he kept in a shoe box loaded with a full clip. Wasting no more time, he hurried back out to the parking lot.

Thankfully, his car was where he'd left it days ago, untouched.

He jumped in, twisted the key, and nothing. He didn't have time for a dead battery. What were the chances he could get someone to jump him this late at night?

The clock was ticking closer to the appointed time. Tuck left his car and hurried through the bushes back to where he'd left Julia parked beneath the tree.

When the tree came in sight, his gut told him something wasn't right. The closer he got to the tree and its low-hanging branches, the faster he moved until he was running.

It didn't matter. The car was still there, but it was empty.

He ducked inside, checked the floorboards, the backseat. Julia was gone.

Standing outside, Tuck did a three-sixty, scanning the streets, hoping she'd only walked away for a moment, tired of sitting still. He knew how stupid the thought was. She wouldn't have left without him without a good reason. Knowing how dangerous these thugs were, it would be suicide to stroll right into their midst and expect them to let her walk away.

The car doors had all been closed and locked when he'd left her. Though unlocked now, there was no indication of forced entry. If the bad guys had come up to the car, they'd have forced the door open or Julia would have tried to drive the car away. Unless they'd pointed a gun at her head, in which case she might have unlocked the doors.

He glanced back inside the car and found the prepaid cell phone lying on the seat. The damaged phone was nowhere in sight. She'd taken it with her.

Tuck's heart sank into his gut. Had she gotten the call

from the kidnappers? His hands shook as he searched the phone history. In the past ten minutes two calls were recorded. One blocked sender coming in and one going out after it. He recognized the one going out as the number to the FBI building. He hit Redial and waited, his hands shaking.

The operator came on and asked how he'd like his call directed.

"Josh Behling." He waited, his foot tapping against the ground. The longer Julia was missing the worse it could be for her. Why had she made the call to the FBI?

"Behling."

"It's Tuck. Did Julia call you or Pierce?"

"Not me. Let me ask Pierce."

A moment passed and Josh spoke. "Not Pierce. Why?"

"She called the FBI building while I was checking out my apartment. I need you to find out who took the most recent call into the building."

"Huh?"

"Just find out."

"Will do. Here, talk to Pierce while I run this information down."

Tuck gripped the phone harder. "Hurry."

"Tuck?"

When Pierce's concerned voice sounded in Tuck's ear, a wash of desperation threatened to overwhelm him. "She's gone."

"What do you mean she's gone?"

"She left while I was arranging for a different car."

Pierce swore. "Do you think she got the call from the kidnappers and is trying to handle it on her own?"

"I'm not sure. She rang the office after she received an incoming call."

"Does she have the phone with the video?"

"Yes." Tuck leaned against car, afraid his wobbly knees wouldn't hold. "Why didn't she stay put?"

"You're asking the wrong person. I've never understood how female minds work. She seemed to like you. Maybe she doesn't want you hurt any more? Wait, here's Josh."

"Tuck?" Josh's voice came across the line. "The operator said she directed a call from a woman asking for the visiting supervisor from Minneapolis. She patched her through to the boss's office."

Tuck straightened. "Are they still there?"

"The boss is. I asked him what the call was all about. He didn't know, just that Mullins took off in a hurry."

"He left?" Tuck shoved the phone beneath his chin, opened the car door and pulled the hood release.

"Yeah," Josh said. "He got a call and left. That's all we know here."

"Anyone go with him?" Tuck asked.

"No one from this office, and he arrived here alone."

Just as sure as he knew his own name, Tuck knew Julia had called in Jillian's supervisor to handle the exchange. But why the guy hadn't taken any backup was beyond Tuck.

A sick feeling settled in his belly. "Get on the phone with the regional tech guru and have him put a trace on Mullins's cell phone. Tell him it's an emergency and Mullins may be in trouble. Tell him anything, just get a GPS coordinate for him in the next two minutes. Put Pierce on." Tuck opened the hood of the rental car, worked the battery cables loose, jerked the battery out of its metal bracket and balanced it on the edge of the car.

"What's going on, Tuck?" Pierce asked.

"Sounds like Julia called in Mullins to make the exchange. As far as anyone knows, he's alone."

"Is he insane? These guys are armed and dangerous."

"I don't know anything about the guy and don't trust anyone with the lives of my wife and daughter."

"Wife?" Tuck could imagine Pierce's brows rising, but he didn't have time to argue. "When Josh finds Mullins, meet me wherever he is. I'm going to need backup. Call me as soon as you find him."

Tuck clicked the off button, grabbed the battery from the rental and ran for his car. He prayed that by the time he installed the battery, Josh or Pierce would call back with the location of Mullins and, hopefully, Julia.

After two minutes, Tuck had the old battery out, the new one in and his car running like a charm. He climbed into the driver's seat, buckled his seat belt and prayed for the phone to ring.

As if on cue, it did.

"Did you get it?" Tuck demanded.

"Got it." Josh rattled off the address. "I've got the trace up on my computer. I'll let you know if he moves. Pierce is on his way. I'd join you, but—"

"I need you on the computer in case Mullins moves."

"What I thought. Stay safe." Josh disconnected. Unfamiliar with the address, Tuck entered it into his GPS and shot out of the parking lot onto the road. In six seconds, he hit sixty, blowing through traffic lights and stop signs as if they weren't there, sending up silent prayers to the Great Spirit to protect his girls.

JULIA HAD LEFT THE CAR and walked to the nearest convenience store, keeping to the shadows as she'd learned from Tuck. No one followed her, and the roads were fairly deserted. Once at the combination gas-and-grocery store, she asked to borrow the telephone.

Five precious minutes later, a taxi arrived. Why Mullins hadn't wanted to pick her up himself was a mystery to her. He'd claimed it would be faster for her to catch a cab and meet him two blocks from where the exchange would take place. She'd hand off the phone to him, let him make the exchange and still be close by to take Lily after the deal was done.

At the time she'd made the arrangement, it made sense. Now, with the taxi slowing to a stop on the dark streets of the industrial and warehouse end of town, Julia was having second thoughts. There wasn't anyone around. No cars, no people, no backup.

"Hey, lady, you sure you want to get out here?" The cab driver looked at her in the rearview mirror.

"I'm…sure." She glanced around, her hand on the door handle. Ten of the fifteen minutes had already passed since the kidnappers had called. With only two blocks between her and her baby, Julia couldn't give up hope now. If Mullins didn't show, she'd do it herself. "Yes. I'm sure."

Julia climbed out and paid the cab driver with the last of the money she'd had when she and Lily had run from her apartment in Fort Yates. She watched as the taxi pulled away, the taillights disappearing around the next corner. Clutching the ruined cell phone in her hand, she wished she'd also brought the prepaid one with her. With only five minutes left to make it the two blocks to the exchange site, she prayed she'd done the right thing.

Seconds after the cab disappeared, headlights blinked on from a narrow street between two large metal buildings.

Her heart hammering, Julia stepped into the shadows of the warehouse next to her and dropped down beside a brick garden box filled with bushes and an array of annual flowers. She crouched beside it and waited, hoping and praying Supervisory Special Agent Mullins had arrived.

As she waited, she rolled the phone in her hands, testing the weight, wondering if the images on it were truly retrievable. The phone represented all they'd gone through—the attempts on their lives, Jillian's sacrifice—all for the identity of who'd killed the NIGC representative. Someone didn't want his identity revealed.

A large, dark SUV, very similar to the ones that had pursued them in Fort Yates, pulled onto the road and crept toward her.

Julia's legs wobbled and her breathing came in short spasms. She huddled in the corner beside the garden box, her pulse pounding so hard against her eardrums she could barely hear. She remained in the shadows, hunkering lower.

What if it wasn't the FBI agent but the kidnappers? Followed closely on that thought was, what if they had Lily in the SUV? Before she could think straight, she jammed the phone into the garden box, slipping it far back beneath the lip of the brick before lurching to her feet. Then she stepped out of the shadows and into the dull yellow glow of a streetlight.

The SUV stopped. The passenger climbed out, leaving the driver in the vehicle. A tall man with gray hair and wearing a dark suit approached. "Julia Anderson?"

Julia nodded. "Yes."

"I'm Supervisory Special Agent Mullins. I was your sister's supervisor before her untimely death. Let me offer my condolences. We'd worked together on a number of cases. She was one of my best." He stuck out his hand.

Julia's heart squeezed, once again reminded of the sister she'd never see again. She took the man's hand and gave it a brief shake. "Thank you for coming."

Mullins reached inside his jacket.

Julia jerked backward, her first instinct to think he might be pulling a gun.

His hands froze and then he raised them in surrender. "I'm just reaching for my wallet."

Julia blew out the breath that had lodged in her throat. After all that had happened, she was punchy and wary. Better that than dead. "Go ahead."

The agent pulled his wallet from inside his breast pocket and flipped it open to display his FBI badge and credentials.

All the tension drained from Julia's body and she nearly cried. One of the good guys. Someone Jillian had worked with. "Thank God."

Mullins glanced around and behind her. "You came alone?"

"Yes. The kidnappers insisted I deliver the phone alone."

Mullins nodded. "Where's Agent Thunder Horse?"

"I left him at his apartment. He didn't need to be involved."

"Why is that? From what I'm told, you two have been inseparable since this all began."

Julia tried to think of a lie, but her nerves were so taut with worry over getting Lily back, she couldn't think of anything but the truth. "He's the father of the baby. I couldn't risk his life and mine and leave Lily parentless."

The supervisor's eyes narrowed. "Are you sure there

are no other witnesses to the murder? Did Agent Thunder Horse or anyone else view the video?"

Julia shook her head. "No one. It all happened so fast. We were on the run…" She shrugged. "I wish I could help you more. I want that bastard to pay for killing my sister."

"Oh, I'm sure he will." Mullins crossed his arms over his chest. "Miss Anderson, did you bring the phone with the video?"

Julia nodded. "It doesn't work. When we were running, I dropped it in the water. I'm not certain if the data on it is even retrievable."

"You tried?"

"Tuck's brother Pierce sent it to someone who specializes in recovering data."

"Were they able to retrieve the video in the Minneapolis office?" Mullins asked.

Julia frowned. Had she mentioned Minneapolis? As far as she'd known, Tuck, Josh and Pierce were the only ones besides the tech guy in Minneapolis who knew that it had gone to the regional office. Tuck had assured her that they'd kept it below the radar, since Jillian had said not to trust anyone. Then who had let it slip to Mullins?

"They didn't have time to download before the killer kidnapped my baby and demanded the phone in exchange. It was all we could do to get it back here in the time frame given." Julia tipped her head. "You have a better inside track into the Minneapolis office. Why didn't you ask the tech guy yourself?"

Mullins gave her half a smile. "I left as soon as I'd heard Agent Anderson had been killed. Anything else?"

"Like what?"

"Were there any others who witnessed the murders

of Agent Anderson and the NIGC representative?" Mullins asked.

"No." Julia glanced toward the vehicle. The windows were tinted dark so that she couldn't see inside. "Shouldn't you be heading to the exchange location?"

"I will in just a minute."

"They'll be there by now with Lily."

"Then I'll need that phone." He held out his hand.

Julia glanced from his hand to the SUV. No one had gotten out. It stood like an ominous monster from a scary movie. Anyone or anything could be inside, and it was beginning to really bother Julia. "I don't have it on me."

Mullins's mild-mannered face turned to stone, his lips pressing together into a very thin line. "You just said you had the phone."

The chilling bite in his voice seemed to drop the temperature to below freezing.

The hairs on Julia's arms rose. "I do, but not exactly on me."

Mullins stepped closer. "Where *exactly* is it?"

"Someplace safe for the moment."

He grabbed her hand, squeezing hard enough to leave a bruise. "I suggest you get it."

Julia stared up into the agent's eyes, fear licking at her insides. "You're hurting me."

He loosened his hold and finally let go, adjusting his suit jacket. "We don't want to keep the kidnappers waiting, do we?"

Julia backed away. "No, we don't. I'll just get it." She turned and moved toward the building, veering away from the garden box and aiming for an alley, her instincts telling her to run.

The sound of a car door opening made her look back.

Two men climbed out of the SUV, both dark-haired, large, muscular, their faces set in tight, mean lines. Julia's heart flipped over when one turned enough that she could see the side of his head. A flash of white streaked through his dark hair.

Her breath hitched and she stumbled. It was him, the man she'd seen shoot the NIGC agent. Before she reached the building or came any closer to the garden box where she'd left the phone, she realized she was trapped. She couldn't run away from this tangle without risking losing Lily forever. If Agent Mullins was in fact the man receiving the kickback from Pickett, he was probably also responsible for kidnapping her daughter. Lily could be in that SUV.

The video on the phone was her only leverage. If she gave it up now, both she and Lily would die.

Julia gathered a deep breath and turned, her shoulders squaring. "You did it, didn't you?"

"A lot like your sister, aren't you?" He nodded, a sneer curling one corner of his lip. "Be careful you don't end up like her."

"She was a good agent. She tried to make the world a better place through her work." Julia's voice caught. "Her only fault was trusting you."

"Stop fooling around, Julia," Mullins warned. "If you want your baby back, we need that phone for the trade."

"You weren't planning on trading anything, were you?" She walked toward him. "You're the one the NIGC rep called the Big Boss, aren't you?"

"That's ridiculous. I'd never met the man." His eyes narrowed. "You're wasting time. Give me the phone." He held out his hand.

"So, you haven't been receiving kickbacks from the NIGC representative, and the man with the white streak in his hair standing by your car wasn't in Fort Yates the day my sister died and didn't kill Pickett...under *your* orders?"

Mullins's face darkened, his eyes narrowing into a squint. He grabbed Julia and pressed the cold metal barrel of a pistol to her temple. "No more games. Where's. The. Phone?"

Chapter Sixteen

Halfway to the warehouse and distribution district, Tuck's phone rang.

It was his brother. "Lights out. You're a mile from the location."

"Done." Tuck slowed and switched off his headlights. The abrupt change left him momentarily night blind. If not for the scattered streetlights, he'd have run off the road. As soon as his night vision kicked in, he increased his speed.

"Tuck?"

"Yeah, Pierce."

"Got some bad news."

Tuck's belly flipped. "I could use some good news about now."

"Sorry, brother."

"Give it to me."

"Skeeter was able to download that video before sending the phone back after all. We have a fairly clear picture of the guy who shot Pickett."

"And?"

"He's an informant by the name of Nat Tendell. The Minneapolis office has used his services on many occasions."

"Informant?"

"Yeah. One agent in particular has been known to use him a lot."

Based on his brother's tone, Tuck knew who that particular agent was, but until he had confirmation from his brother he prayed it wasn't so. "Who?"

"Supervisory Special Agent Ray Mullins. Mullins also had some assault charges against Tendell expunged from his records a month ago."

Tuck's foot slipped off the accelerator. "Mullins and Tendell are working this together, aren't they?"

"Looks that way."

"Mullins is the Big Boss and Tendell is one of his enforcers?"

"Skeeter did more digging under the table and found some dirt."

"On Mullins?"

"Yup. Seems he's made a few transfers from a bank in the Caymans to an account stateside."

"Let me guess, from Pickett's account to Tendell's account." Tuck prayed to the Great Spirit. "Julia's walking into a trap."

"In a big way," Pierce agreed. "I'm almost there."

"I hope we're not too late."

Tuck had agreed to come in from the north, Pierce from the south. They'd park a couple of blocks from the address Josh had given them and sneak in.

Two streets away, Tuck parked his car against the side of the road and got out, shutting the door quietly. Then he ran as fast as he could, ignoring the pain in his leg as he kept to the shadows of the buildings. He headed directly for the coordinates Josh had given him, carrying his SIG Sauer up front and ready.

Finally, he reached the back of the building that faced the street address where Mullins had stopped. A dark silhouette appeared at the corner of the building one over from him. The shadowy figure gave a brief wave.

Pierce. Tuck's backup had arrived. Knowing his brother was with him on this gave him added confidence.

Inching along the wall of the building, he moved toward the front. Voices carried into the night, growing louder the closer he came to the street. He caught some of the words.

"The man with the white streak in his hair standing by your car wasn't in Fort Yates the day my sister died and didn't kill Pickett...under *your* orders?"

Immediately Tuck knew it was Julia's voice and she was angry, accusing someone of murder. Her courage and spunkiness made his chest swell with pride, though simultaneously his gut clenched at the amount of danger she faced.

Tuck forced himself not to run out into the open and storm the agent until he had a take on the situation. Edging to the corner, he peered around.

Mullins had Julia in a neck lock, his government-issue weapon pressed to her head.

Tuck's heart bounced to the bottom of his belly and back into his throat. She was in trouble, big trouble, but somehow he'd get her out of it. He had to. He realized he'd loved that woman since the day he'd married her. Tuck would do anything to keep Mullins from hurting Julia.

"Where's the phone?" Mullins demanded.

"I gave it to the satellite-office manager," Julia lied.

"No, you didn't."

"Are you sure?" Julia asked, her hands clawing at the arm around her throat.

Mullins snorted. "You wouldn't do that knowing your daughter's life is in the balance."

Julia's hands stilled. "Speaking of which…where is she? Where's Lily?"

"Did you think I was stupid? That I could trust you to do exactly what I said?" He squeezed harder. "She's somewhere you won't find her until it's too late. Give me the phone and I'll tell you where that is."

Tuck saw a movement behind the SUV.

It was Pierce slipping up on Tendell. He grabbed the enforcer from behind in a powerful headlock. Tendell's hands waved wildly and a shot fired into the air.

Mullins spun, keeping his hold on Julia.

At the same time, Tuck fired a shot, hitting the second enforcer in the shoulder. The man jerked back, slammed into the car and slid to the ground.

Tuck stepped into the open and shouted, "Mullins, let her go."

"Tuck!" Julia cried.

Pierce had jammed his weapon to Tendell's head. "Drop it, or I drop you. Trust me, you're going to take a big fall this time. Mullins won't get you out of a murder charge."

"Don't listen to him. We have the upper hand," Mullins shouted. "We have the girl and the baby."

"You're an idiot if you put all your trust in a crooked agent. He'll bail on you and let you take the fall for him."

Tendell struggled and fired off another round.

"Forget this." Pierce grunted and tightened his hold around Tendell's neck, leaning back, pulling the killer's feet off the ground.

The man's face darkened and finally his entire body went still.

Pierce loosened his hold just enough for the man to breathe.

Tuck let go of the breath he'd held as the man's weapon dropped to the pavement. Pierce eased the man to the ground, checked his pulse, then pulled his arms behind his back, slapped a plastic zip tie around his wrists and cinched it tight.

Pierce glanced up to Mullins. "Don't worry. He'll live to testify."

"It's over, Mullins." Tuck moved closer. "Right now your boss is viewing the video of Pickett's murder at Fort Yates."

"So? What does it prove? Tendell did it."

Tendell stirred beneath Pierce's hold. "You son of a bitch," he muttered. "You paid me to do your dirty work."

"You can't prove it."

"You're wrong." Tuck stepped closer. "Skeeter has been putting in some overtime and he's been working wonders at hacking. You should know—you hired him."

Mullins stiffened. "I have nothing to hide."

"Except the Cayman bank account you've been moving money in and out of. Money you used to pay our talented Mr. Tendell here." Tuck nodded toward Julia. "Let her go and I'll tell them you cooperated."

"No way." Mullins's hold tightened around Julia's neck. "She's my ticket out of here."

"You aren't going anywhere." Tuck took another step.

Mullins pressed the barrel of the gun to Julia's cheek. "Any closer and I'll shoot her."

"Then you wouldn't have a hostage, and I'd kill you." Tuck's voice dropped low and menacing as he continued to point his gun at Mullins's chest.

Mullins turned Julia, placing her between Tuck and

himself, using her as a human shield. "I want a plane and clearance to get out of this country. When I get where I'm going safely, I'll release her."

Tuck shook his head. "One of the first things I learned in the FBI is that we don't negotiate with terrorists."

"Are you forgetting about the baby?" Mullins slid his cheek against Julia's hair. "I'll bet the girl hasn't, have you, darling?"

"Bastard," Julia gasped.

Tuck shot a glance at Pierce. "Check the SUV."

Mullins snorted. "You don't think I'd bring the biggest bargaining chip I had to the party, now, do you?"

With one foot planted in the middle of his prisoner's back, Pierce yanked open the SUV doors and checked inside. When he turned to Tuck, he shook his head.

Tuck's chest squeezed tighter, rage building in a surge of heat. "Where is she?"

"Anything happens to me, I won't tell you. By the time you find her, she'll be dead."

Julia gasped. "You wouldn't hurt an innocent baby."

"I wouldn't be the one hurting her. It's totally up to you. Your call." He smiled. "Now, do I get my plane? I figure the baby won't last many days without care. Make it a fast plane and get it here in the next hour, or I start shooting Miss Anderson, one limb at a time."

Anger burned so hot, Tuck's hands shook, his finger pressing harder on the trigger. If he didn't keep a lid on his temper the gun would go off.

"Shoot him, Tuck," Julia begged. "Shoot him. He deserves to die for what he did to my sister."

"I can't, baby." Tuck shook his head. "I might hit you."

"You can find Lily. I know you will." Light glinted off the tears welling in her eyes.

Tuck's heart hurt for her and for his child. There had to be a way out of this without killing Julia or letting Lily die.

"Shoot him," Julia pleaded.

"Shut up." Mullins slapped the side of her head with the barrel of his gun.

Julia winced, a trickle of blood slipping down from where he'd broken the skin.

Tuck lunged forward.

"Don't, Tuck," Pierce said. "He's playing you, trying to force your hand."

"It's working," Tuck growled. "If I get half a chance, I'm gonna kill him." Tuck was breathing hard, the blood surging through his veins so fast he might explode. Then he looked into Julia's eyes.

All the terror had been replaced with something else. Cool, deadly determination. She captured his gaze. "I love you, Tuck Thunder Horse. If you love me, you'll shoot."

Tuck held his gun steady. She loved him. Julia loved him.

His mind grew crystal clear and he aimed down the barrel, his target in line.

Julia's chest rose and fell, then she jabbed her elbow hard into Mullins's gut. The surprise of her attack made him lose his grip. She ducked out of his hold, dropping to the ground.

As if the world swung into slow motion, Mullins straightened, his gun rising with him.

Tuck's breathing evened out and he squeezed the trigger.

The bullet hit Mullins in the chest. He fell backward, his own gun falling from his fingers and clattering against the pavement.

Julia rolled onto her hands and knees and crawled over to Mullins, grabbing him by the lapels of his jacket, soaking her hands in his blood. "Where is she, you bastard?" Julia sobbed. "Where is my baby?"

Tuck raced to her side and pulled her off Mullins. He leaned close to the man. "You're going to die anyway. Do something decent before you kick it, and tell us where Lily is."

Mullins stared up at Tuck, a smile curling the corners of his lips. "You'll never find her…" he whispered, then his face went slack and he ceased breathing.

Tuck grabbed him by the collar and shook him. "Where is she, dammit!"

"He's dead," Pierce said. "But we have his henchman." Pierce dragged Tendell to his feet.

Tuck jumped up and stood toe-to-toe with the killer. "Tell us or I'll shoot you like I shot Mullins."

Tendell shrugged. "I don't much care for killin' babies, but I don't know where the kid is. Mullins took care of her after we snatched her in Hazen."

Tuck turned to his brother, hope leaching out of him with every passing minute.

"I'm sure he'd have used her as a bargaining tool if he knew where she was." Pierce confirmed what Tuck had already concluded in his own mind.

Julia rose, her eyes round, filled with tears. "We have to find her."

Tuck pulled his phone out of his pocket and dialed a number in Minneapolis. "Skeeter, I need one more big favor."

JULIA LEANED INTO TUCK as they entered the only hotel in a small North Dakota town an hour north of Bismarck. If they were wrong about this, they'd have to start all over. It had taken three hours to come up with the information that had led them to this particular spot fifty miles away from Bismarck in a community big enough to support only a couple of churches and a handful of houses.

"She'll be here," Tuck reassured her for the hundredth time since they'd piled into the car and raced north from Bismarck.

Julia had begun to think he was saying the words to reassure himself, as well. They'd notified the sheriff of the county but had climbed into the car in Bismarck and left before they'd gotten word back. Once outside Bismarck all cell-phone reception had been dropped.

When they arrived in the little town, they'd gone straight to the hotel and asked for the room number for Ray Mullins. The sleepy desk clerk had taken one look at Tuck's badge and jerked the paper files from beneath the counter.

Julia leaned up on her toes to peer over the counter, straining to see the names on the papers. Lily could be steps away from her. Her pulse jerked fast, slow, fast again. The roller coaster of emotional ups and downs was wearing on her.

"Ray Mullins," the clerk repeated to himself. "I just came on my shift thirty minutes ago, could have checked in during the day—not that we get many people swarming the place unless there's a rodeo in town."

Julia's fingers dug into the countertop and she bit down hard on her tongue to keep from yelling at the young man to shut up and find the room.

"I don't remember that name. Ray you said?" The

clerk's hand paused in the middle of the file and pulled out a single sheet. "How about an R. Mullins?"

"Yes!" Julia dropped back on her feet, clasping and unclasping her hands. "That has to be it."

"Room 207." The clerk turned to a set of numbered wooden boxes behind him and searched through. "That's funny. The spare key isn't here."

"That's because I gave it to the sheriff." An older woman stepped behind the counter, rubbing sleep from her eyes. She smiled at Julia and Tuck. "Sorry, he was in here almost an hour ago and hasn't come back with the key. He might still be there, although I didn't see his car in the driveway."

The young male clerk shrugged. "He could have walked. The station is only a block away."

"I'll go check the room," the woman said.

Julia shook her head, already halfway out the door. "Don't bother. We will and if they're not there, we'll go over to the sheriff's office."

What started as a swift walk became an all-out run. Julia raced along the building, searching for room 207. "Where is it?"

"Take the stairs. It's on the second floor." Tuck reached the staircase before she did and took the steps two at a time.

Julia followed, breathing hard by the time she reached the top.

Tuck stopped at the first door to the right, his hand on the doorknob. "Everything's going to be all right." He twisted the knob and pushed.

The door didn't open.

Julia reached around Tuck and knocked.

No answer.

"If you're lookin' for the sheriff, he left a few minutes ago," a woman called from below in the parking lot.

Julia leaned over the rail. "You saw him?"

The woman nodded. "Talked to him, too."

"Was he alone?" Julia asked, her voice tight.

"He was when he arrived, but he wasn't when he left." The woman sighed. "Let me guess. You're the baby's mama."

Julia's eyes filled with tears. "Baby? Oh, God, he has my baby." She ran to the stairs and had to blink several times before she could start down.

Tuck's hand on her arm steadied her and they descended together.

When they reached the bottom, Julia rushed forward and clasped the woman's hands. "You saw Lily?"

"That's her name?" The woman smiled. "I saw her, held her, played with her and took care of her for part of the day and half the night." The woman squeezed Julia's hands. "I'm so sorry. The sheriff told me about the kidnapping. I didn't know. The gentleman seemed nice. He told me he was the baby's grandfather. Paid me two hundred dollars to keep her until he got back from a business trip. I didn't think anything of it until the sheriff showed up."

Julia stared into the woman's eyes. "Was she okay? Did she cry much?"

"Best baby I've ever babysat." The woman squeezed her hand and let go. "You better go get her. No tellin' how the sheriff is doing at changin' diapers."

Julia started to take off and was jerked to a stop when a large hand grabbed her elbow.

Tuck grinned. "Wrong way." He turned her in the opposite direction and held her hand, power walking with her the one block to the sheriff's office.

When she pushed through the door, the overwhelming surge of love and relief almost brought her to her knees.

The sheriff sat behind a desk, rocking Lily.

When they walked in, he glanced up and smiled. "Miss Anderson?"

Julia gulped on the rush of tears and nodded. "Yes, sir."

"Lily and I have been waiting on you, and your timing is perfect. I think she needs a fresh diaper." The sheriff stood and rounded the desk. "Sure glad we were able to find the little one for you."

"Me, too, Sheriff. Me, too." Julia took Lily in her arms and hugged her to her chest, tears running down her cheeks.

Tuck reached across and shook the sheriff's hand. "Thank you for helping out."

"She's a cute little thing." The sheriff nodded toward the baby and looked up at Tuck. "Looks just like her daddy. She'll have you wrapped around her little finger so fast you won't know what hit you."

Tuck grinned, slipping his arm around Julia and Lily. "She already has."

Julia leaned into Tuck as he led them out of the sheriff's office and back the way they'd come to the hotel and his car. Once they had the baby buckled into the car seat, Julia climbed in the backseat with her.

She didn't want to let Lily out of her sight ever again.

"Where to?" Tuck asked.

"I don't care." Julia's voice cracked on a fresh wave of grateful tears. "I have Lily."

"Going back to Fort Yates?" Tuck asked.

Julia slid a finger along the baby's cheek. "I can't. I

know I need to take care of Jillian's funeral, but I just can't go back there."

"We can make arrangements to have her funeral elsewhere." Tuck glanced at her in the rearview mirror. "I know the perfect place for you now. Do you trust me?"

Julia met his gaze without blinking. "With my life and with Lily's."

"Then settle in. It'll take a couple hours to get there."

Chapter Seventeen

Tuck stood on the porch, staring out at the soft prairie grasses waving in the breeze. It felt good to be home on the Thunder Horse Ranch. He could finally relax and take it easy. Well, almost. First he had to settle things with Julia.

An arm slipped around him, squeezing his waist.

He glanced down at his mother.

She smiled, happier than he'd seen her since the death of his father. "She's beautiful."

"Julia?"

Her chuckle warmed the chill morning air. "And Lily." Her arm tightened around his middle. "Why didn't you tell us?"

"I don't know. It all happened so fast and was over within a couple days. It didn't seem real."

"I'm a grandmother." His mother sighed. "And she looks like a Thunder Horse. Have you two thought about where you're going to live? Your apartment is too small for the three of you."

"Slow down, Mom. I have to convince Julia we belong together."

His mother's brows rose. "It's obvious. You love her, don't you?"

Tuck stared out at the prairie. "More than anything."

"Then tell her."

"It's not that simple." Tuck disengaged from his mother's embrace and leaned against a porch column. "She doesn't want to be married to anyone working with the FBI."

His mother nodded. "It's a scary life for a woman to watch a loved one leave for work, never knowing if he'll come back alive."

"Exactly. Her father and her sister have both died working for the FBI. How can I convince her that won't happen to me?"

Amelia faced the prairie. "You can't. Life doesn't come with guarantees. Who would have thought your father would fall off his horse and die?"

Tuck's eyes narrowed. He still wasn't convinced his father fell off his horse, but that was another argument, long since past. "If I want to keep Julia and Lily in my life, I have to do some fancy talking."

"Not fancy. Just sincere." Amelia laid a hand on his chest. "Speak from your heart."

"What if it's not enough?" He knew he'd see Lily again. Julia had told him as much. Still, his chest ached at the thought of losing the woman who'd stolen his heart from the first time they'd met.

JULIA STOOD BEHIND the screen door, shamelessly eavesdropping on the conversation on the porch. More than once she started to clear her throat and announce her presence, but each time, Tuck had said something else that made her hesitate, until she hung on every word.

They'd arrived during the early-morning hours, the sky still filled with so many stars, Julia could spend the rest of her life counting and never get them all.

The ranch house had been warm and inviting, Tuck's

mother and brother Maddox welcoming her like family. Never had she felt more at home than on the Thunder Horse Ranch, surrounded by a family who obviously cared about each other.

Amelia Thunder Horse had been so excited by the news that she was a grandmother that Julia hadn't found it in her heart to tell her that she would be seeing Lily only when Tuck had visitation.

Julia stared through the haze of screen at the man who'd moved heaven and earth to protect her and Lily. He'd been willing to give his life for them—and almost had.

Her heart flipped in her chest at the fresh memories of their ordeal. All of that was in the past, even if it would live on as nightmares for months to come.

One truth rose out of it all. Julia loved Tuck Thunder Horse. She'd been silly and slightly drunk when she'd married him after knowing him only a night, claiming it was love at first sight. Now she knew. It was love at every sight with Tuck.

He was everything she could have hoped for in a man. She'd been drawn to him for all the attributes she'd loved most in her father and sister. Strength of character, courage and a sense of duty that extended to those who couldn't protect themselves.

Why hadn't she seen that before? She loved Tuck because he was like her father and sister, and yet she'd pushed him away for the same reason. What a fool she'd been.

With no plan, no course of action thoroughly thought through, Julia pushed through the door, determined to correct the huge mistake she'd made. The sooner the better.

"Am I interrupting?" Julia asked.

Amelia turned a bright smile her way. "Not at all, dear. I was just about to go prepare lunch." She hugged Julia and patted her cheek. "Have I said thank-you for bringing my granddaughter to me?"

Julia laughed. "At least three times now." She hugged Tuck's mother, her smile fading. "I'm sorry I kept her from you for so long."

"Not to worry. I can hold and cuddle her now. Which I'm planning to do before I head for the kitchen." Amelia slipped past Julia and into the house, leaving the two of them alone on the porch.

Silence stretched as Julia struggled for a starting point. Tuck didn't utter a word, not making it any easier. "Where's Maddox?" she finally blurted.

"He and his fiancée, Katya, rode out this morning. He wanted to show her the wild horses of the canyon."

"I'd love to see the horses." Julia faced Tuck. "Will you take me?"

"If you stay long enough." He continued to stare out at the landscape, refusing to look at her.

"I'd like to." Julia laid her hand on his arm. "Tuck?"

He looked down at where her hand lay. "I'm not good at this."

"At what?" she asked.

He covered her hand with his. "Finding the right words."

"Then let me."

"No, I need to say this." He gripped her arms and stared into her eyes. "But I have to get it right."

"Okay." She raised her hand to cup his cheek. "I'm listening."

"Mom said to speak from my heart. Well, here it is, plain and simple." He took a deep breath. "I love you,

Julia Anderson. If you want me to give up the FBI to be with you, so be it. I'll quit today."

"Tuck—"

He pressed a finger to her lips. "Let me finish."

She nodded, smiling against his finger.

"It took almost losing you to realize you're more important to me than saving the world. I want you to marry me…again. And I want you and Lily to live with me. We can be a family. I'll be a good dad to Lily and a good husband to you." His lips curved. "You'll make that part easy, because you're both so darned easy to love." He stared at her, his gaze intense, burning a hole straight through her heart. "Julia, will you marry me? Please?"

She laughed, releasing the remaining worry from her heart and embracing all the joy of life. "Tuck Thunder Horse…" Her hands framed his face and pulled him closer. "I love you more than all the stars in the North Dakota sky. I want to spend the rest of my life with you, and I want Lily to know how great her *FBI special agent* father is."

He shook his head. "But I won't be an agent. I'm giving it up."

"Not if you want to be with me, you're not. I realized that that part of you is what made me fall in love with you. It's who you are, just like it was who my father and sister were. You're a man who wants to make the world a safer place. You can't change that, and I wouldn't want you to."

Tuck pulled her into his arms and kissed her soundly, then pushed her away, a frown forming. "Just one thing."

"What's that?"

"You never answered my question."

Julia chuckled. "I didn't?"

"No." He dropped down on one knee and took her

hand in his. "Maybe I didn't ask it the right way. Julia Anderson, I love you with all my heart. Will you marry me?"

"Can we invite Marshall and Lois Glimm to the wedding?"

"Anyone you want to invite is fine by me."

Julia squeezed his fingers, her heart so full it threatened to overflow in tears. "In that case...yes, Tuck Thunder Horse...I'll marry you...again."

"Using the word of a brave bush pilot—" Tuck stood and yelled, "Yeehaw!" Then he swung Julia up in his arms and set her back on her feet. "We're going to do it right this time. Can we do it in fourteen days?"

Breathless, Julia grinned. "It only took a day before. Two weeks will be overkill."

"A week it is." Then Tuck kissed her, and Julia knew they'd be doing a whole lot more of that before and after the wedding.

Amelia Thunder Horse carried Lily out onto the porch. "Someone wants her mama." She handed Lily to Julia, but the baby leaned toward Tuck instead.

Julia laughed and stood aside as Tuck gathered his daughter into his arms. "Mom, we have a wedding to plan."

"Bless the spirits." Amelia clapped her hands together. "When?"

Tuck grinned. "One week."

Julia laughed at how wide Tuck's mother's eyes got.

"Well, then I guess I'd best get busy." Amelia ducked back inside, leaving Tuck, Julia and Lily alone.

Tuck balanced Lily on one arm and slid his other one around Julia. "Think you can handle being a part of this big, crazy family? My mother will smother you, and my brothers can be overwhelming at times."

Julia leaned into his body. "They're a part of you. What's not to love? I love you, Tuck Thunder Horse." She leaned up on her toes and pressed a kiss to his lips.

His arm tightened around her and he kissed her back while Lily cooed happily, nestled between them.

* * * * *

You can find more information on upcoming Harlequin® titles, free excerpts and more at www.Harlequin.com.

HICNM0612

REQUEST YOUR FREE BOOKS!
2 FREE NOVELS PLUS 2 FREE GIFTS!

Harlequin®

INTRIGUE®

BREATHTAKING ROMANTIC SUSPENSE

YES! Please send me 2 FREE Harlequin Intrigue® novels and my 2 FREE gifts (gifts are worth about $10). After receiving them, if I don't wish to receive any more books, I can return the shipping statement marked "cancel." If I don't cancel, I will receive 6 brand-new novels every month and be billed just $4.49 per book in the U.S. or $5.24 per book in Canada. That's a saving of at least 14% off the cover price! It's quite a bargain! Shipping and handling is just 50¢ per book in the U.S. and 75¢ per book in Canada.* I understand that accepting the 2 free books and gifts places me under no obligation to buy anything. I can always return a shipment and cancel at any time. Even if I never buy another book, the two free books and gifts are mine to keep forever.

182/382 HDN FEQ2

Name _____ (PLEASE PRINT) _____

Address _____ Apt. # _____

City _____ State/Prov. _____ Zip/Postal Code _____

Signature (if under 18, a parent or guardian must sign) _____

Mail to the **Reader Service:**
IN U.S.A.: P.O. Box 1867, Buffalo, NY 14240-1867
IN CANADA: P.O. Box 609, Fort Erie, Ontario L2A 5X3
Not valid for current subscribers to Harlequin Intrigue books.

**Are you a subscriber to Harlequin Intrigue books
and want to receive the larger-print edition?
Call 1-800-873-8635 or visit www.ReaderService.com.**

* Terms and prices subject to change without notice. Prices do not include applicable taxes. Sales tax applicable in N.Y. Canadian residents will be charged applicable taxes. Offer not valid in Quebec. This offer is limited to one order per household. All orders subject to credit approval. Credit or debit balances in a customer's account(s) may be offset by any other outstanding balance owed by or to the customer. Please allow 4 to 6 weeks for delivery. Offer available while quantities last.

Your Privacy—The Reader Service is committed to protecting your privacy. Our Privacy Policy is available online at www.ReaderService.com or upon request from the Reader Service.

We make a portion of our mailing list available to reputable third parties that offer products we believe may interest you. If you prefer that we not exchange your name with third parties, or if you wish to clarify or modify your communication preferences, please visit us at www.ReaderService.com/consumerchoice or write to us at Reader Service Preference Service, P.O. Box 9062, Buffalo, NY 14269. Include your complete name and address.

HI11B

*Harlequin Intrigue® presents a new installment
in* USA TODAY *bestselling author
Delores Fossen's miniseries*
THE LAWMEN OF SILVER CREEK RANCH.

Enjoy a sneak peek at KADE.

Kade saw it then. The clear bassinet on rollers, the kind
they used in the hospital nursery.

He walked closer and looked inside. There was a baby,
and it was likely a girl, since there was a pink blanket snuggled around her. There was also a little pink stretchy cap on
her head. She was asleep, but her mouth was puckered as if
sucking a bottle.

"What does the baby have to do with this?" Kade asked.

"Everything. Two days ago someone abandoned her in the
E.R. waiting room," the doctor explained. "The person left
her in an infant carrier next to one of the chairs. We don't
know who did that, because we don't have security cameras."

Kade was finally able to release the breath he'd been
holding. So this was job related. They'd called him in because he was an FBI agent.

But he immediately rethought that.

"An abandoned baby isn't a federal case," Kade clarified,
though Grayson already knew that. Kade reached down and
brushed his index finger over a tiny dark curl that peeked
out from beneath the cap. "You think she was kidnapped or
something?"

When neither the doctor nor Grayson answered, Kade
looked back at them. The anger began to boil through him.
"Did someone hurt her?"

"No," the doctor quickly answered. "There wasn't a
scratch on her. She's perfectly healthy as far as I can tell."

HIEXP0712

The anger went as quickly as it had come. Kade had handled the worst of cases, but the one thing he couldn't stomach was anyone harming a child.

"I called Grayson as soon as she was found," the doctor went on. "There were no Amber Alerts, no reports of missing newborns. There wasn't a note in her carrier, only a bottle that had no prints, no fibers or anything else to distinguish it."

Kade lifted his hands palms up. "That's a lot of no's. What do you know about her?" Because he was sure this was leading somewhere.

Dr. Mickelson glanced at the baby. "We know she's about three or four days old, which means she was abandoned either the day she was born or shortly after. She's slightly underweight, barely five pounds, but there was no hospital bracelet. We had no other way to identify her, so we ran a DNA test." His explanation stopped cold, and his attention came back to Kade.

So did Grayson's. "Kade, she's yours."

How does Kade react when he finds out the baby is his?

Find out in KADE.
Available this July wherever books are sold.